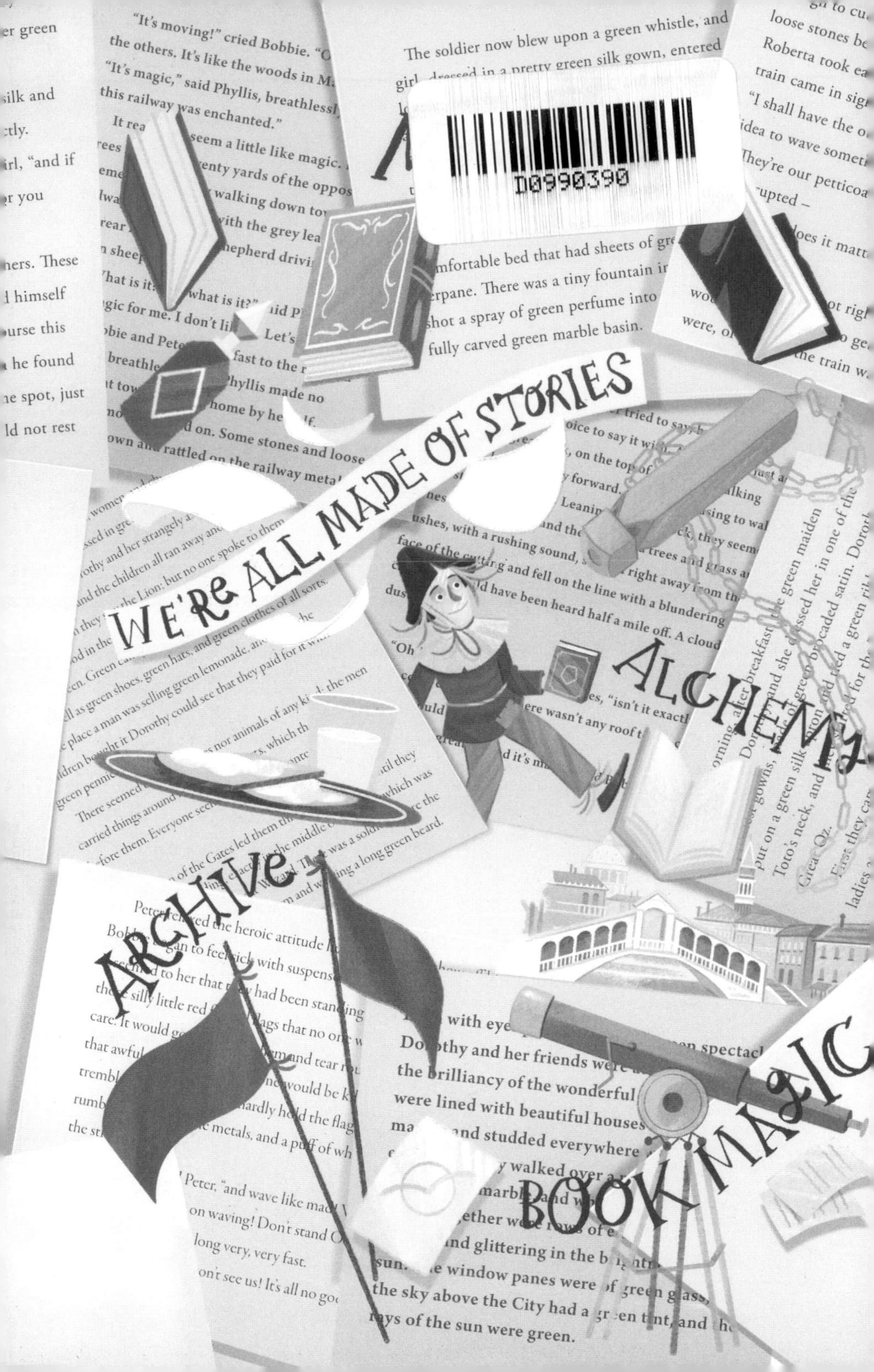

WE'RE ALL MADE OF STORIES
ALCHEMY
ARCHIVE
BOOK MAGIC

PAGES
AND CO.
THE
BOOK SMUGGLERS

The Pages & Co. series

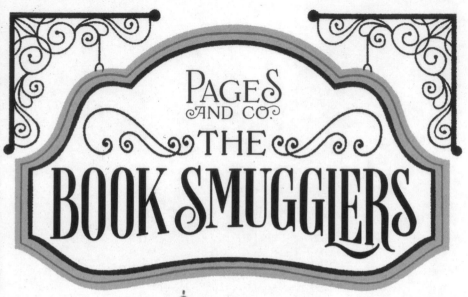

PAGES AND CO.
THE
BOOK SMUGGLERS

ANNA JAMES

ILLUSTRATED BY
MARCO GUADALUPI

PHILOMEL BOOKS

An imprint of Penguin Random House LLC, New York

First published in the United States of America by Philomel Books,
an imprint of Penguin Random House LLC, 2021
First published in Great Britain by HarperCollins Children's Books, 2021

Text copyright © 2021 by Anna James
Illustrations copyright © 2021 by Marco Guadalupi

Visit us online at penguinrandomhouse.com.

Library of Congress Cataloging-in-Publication Data is available.
Book manufactured in Canada
ISBN 9780593327203

1 3 5 7 9 10 8 6 4 2

FRI

US edition edited by Cheryl Eissing • US edition designed by Ellice M. Lee.
Text set in Adobe Caslon.

For my nephew Milo,
who knows the power of book magic.

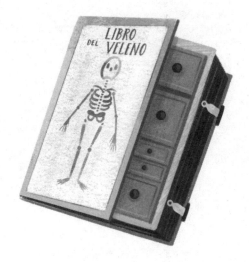

PAGES
AND CO.

THE
BOOK SMUGGLERS

Prologue

The book arrived at Pages & Co. wrapped in brown paper and string. It was addressed to Archibald Pages and covered in a colorful array of mismatched stamps. Archibald's granddaughter, Tilly, had picked up the bundle of post that morning and brought it through from the bookshop the Pages owned to their private family kitchen. Archie didn't notice it until the shop had closed its doors and he was sitting with a cup of tea, sorting through the stack of bills, letters, and books sent from publishers.

"What's this then?" he asked, turning the package over in his hands. It had been wrapped very precisely, with the brown paper in sharp creases, only a little tattered from its journey.

"It was just in with the post," Tilly said. "Are you expecting something exciting?"

"Not that I can remember," Archie

replied. "Although this does *look* rather exciting, doesn't it? The stamps would seem to suggest it's from . . . Italy, I think? How curious." He took out his penknife and neatly sliced through the tape at one end, peeling back the paper with the satisfying crinkling noise that comes from brown paper in particular. Archie pulled out a hardback book that was rather worse for wear—its dark-green cloth cover was frayed at the edges, and several of the pages were visibly ripped and stained. On its spine, in faded gilt lettering, was the book's title, *Il meraviglioso mago di Oz*, and its author, L. Frank Baum.

"An Italian edition of *The Wizard of Oz*," Archie said appreciatively, stroking the edges of the pages in admiration. "I was right about the stamps. But I don't think we know anyone in Italy—do we, Elsie?"

He directed this last question to his wife, Tilly's grandma, as she entered the kitchen.

"I don't think so," she said. 'Is that something you've ordered online and forgotten about again?"

"Not this time," Archie grinned.

"Did it come with a note?" Tilly asked.

"Good thinking," Archie said, opening the cover to

reveal a small rectangular card. All that was on it was a symbol printed in black ink: a circle with a line that crossed it horizontally with a dip in its center, like the outline of a flying bird, or a simple drawing of an open book. Archie turned it over, but there was nothing else printed on it.

"How strange," he said, turning carefully through the pages but not finding anything else tucked inside. "I've never seen this symbol before; it doesn't mean anything to me."

He stood up and started rifling through the rest of the post to see if there was anything else that had come from Italy, but it was just the book and the card. Archie sat down heavily, his face pale.

"Goodness, you look exhausted," Elsie said, coming over and putting a cool hand on his forehead. "And you're burning up." It was a warm day but nowhere near hot enough to produce the rapidly gathering beads of sweat on Archie's skin.

"Just overworked, I'm sure," Archie reassured her. "I'm not getting any younger after all! But I do feel a bit peculiar, now you come to mention it—maybe I'll just have a quick lie-down."

He stood up but quickly wobbled on his feet, and Elsie had to help him up the stairs to their bedroom.

"He fell straight asleep," Elsie said when she returned to the kitchen, looking worried. "And something else strange . . . As I put him to bed, I noticed that his fingertips were purple."

"Purple!" Tilly repeated in surprise.

"Yes, as though he'd been picking blackberries. I wonder if he's touched something he's allergic to . . ." She tailed off as both she and Tilly turned to stare at the mysterious book lying on the table.

Elsie gingerly picked up the brown paper it had come in.

"But he can't be allergic to paper or books or anything like that, can he?" Tilly asked. "Surely he'd know that already, what with working in a bookshop and all."

"The book looks very old," Elsie pointed out. "Perhaps it has some kind of glue that he's sensitive to, or it's come into contact with something unpleasant somehow?"

"But not on purpose?" Tilly asked nervously.

"Goodness, no," Elsie said. "I mean, surely not." She paused and glanced worriedly at Tilly. "Although he does know how to get people riled up," she went on. "And, well, it's not as though we haven't made more than our fair share of enemies in the bookwandering world over the years. But no, who on earth would be sending your grandad something poisonous or dangerous?"

But Tilly wasn't convinced, and she could see by the look on her grandma's face that neither was Elsie.

"Well, let's just put this somewhere safe," Elsie said briskly, picking up the book with some kitchen tongs and sliding it into a large plastic sandwich bag. "And when Archie wakes up, we can see if he has any idea who he's irritated this time."

But, two weeks later,

he was still

a s l e e p .

MILO

1

A Pretty Good Hero

Milo Bolt had read a lot of books and he knew that, on paper at least, he made for a pretty good hero. He had so much in common with so many of the people he read adventures about: his parents had died tragically young, and the circumstances around this event were strange and secret; he was now looked after by an uncle who seemed to barely tolerate him, and he lived on a magical train that tracked down lost and forgotten books.

However, despite all of this, he couldn't help but always feel like a side character, even in his own story.

Potentially, this had something to do with the first six years of his life, which had been spent in an unofficial orphanage in Northumberland at the home of Mr.

and Mrs. Marter, where it was very much frowned upon to develop any grand ideas. Mr. and Mrs. Marter had taken in Milo and four other children who had lost their families to bookwandering accidents, which would be too hard to explain to the authorities. It would be unfair to describe Mr. and Mrs. Marter as cruel, but they could not in good faith be called kind. They did not think it was wise to encourage the children to think too much about hopes and dreams or other things they were unlikely to find.

And so, by age six, all Milo really knew was his name—and then his uncle Horatio had turned up. It had been a dark and stormy night in Northumberland, and without much explanation, Horatio had taken Milo with him to live on the Quip, his train. Despite living onboard an if-not-illegal-then-definitely-unofficial train fueled by imagination, his uncle discouraged Milo from too much bookwandering or too much of anything else apart from helping out on the train. Milo had learned his parents' names, but not much else, and somehow found that he was even lonelier than when he had been with Mr. and Mrs. Marter. He had never been told why Horatio had only come for him when he was six, although he had some theories, including temporary amnesia, various administrative errors, and flaws in the postal service.

Currently, Milo was sitting in his tiny carriage near the back of the train, reading a book about dragons and a secret portal in a mountain, but was torn away from it by the jangle of a bell in the corner of his cabin. Its ring was slightly off-kilter because on one side the bell hit his bed as there was so little space. Everything seemed to jangle against everything else most of the time.

But the bell meant that Horatio needed him, so Milo put a bookmark between the pages of his book and went to find his uncle.

Milo picked his way along the train to Horatio's office, through carriages packed with weird and wonderful books and manuscripts, including one with a huge printing press taking up most of the space and another with a wide table covered in scissors and thread, paper and fabric, where Horatio restored damaged books.

In between the private carriages and the dining car, where any paying travelers or clients gathered, were a small number of luxurious guest quarters, connected by a corridor. There were only three, to minimize the chances of rival book collectors running into each other and, in Horatio's words, to "curate an aura of exclusivity." It was almost always quicker to travel the length of the Quip on its roof, but Milo loved peeking at the fancy rooms: one stately and grand, decorated in velvet and gold, one elegant and calm, with white linen and pale wood, and one warm and decadent, covered in embroidered silk and tasseled lamps.

After those was the dining car, and there, sitting at a wide table with a steaming cup of black coffee, was his uncle. Even though Horatio never acknowledged it, Milo knew the family resemblance was striking. They had the same warm brown skin and dark brown eyes and the same very dark-brown curly hair, although Horatio's was streaked with gray.

"There you are," Horatio said, without looking up. "What took you so long?"

"I came as soon as I heard the bell," Milo said, but he was used to Horatio and the fact that nothing was ever quick or good or clean enough for him, and he had learned to try not to take it personally.

"We've had a new order in," Horatio said. "From the Botanist. She's heard about some sort of secret poison compendium that she wants to track down. The exact form it takes—a cabinet or book or box maybe—she's unclear on, but it must be some sort of clever container, perhaps disguised to look like something else. Whatever its outward appearances, it's hidden somewhere difficult to reach, and so she's willing to pay very generously for it to be recovered. I understand some of the ingredients she hopes to find there might be key to her current research. Sounds like quite the clever artifact."

The Botanist was a regular client, although Milo had never met or seen her; he didn't really get to meet or see anyone. She often hired Horatio to track down dangerous and exciting things to do with plants and poisons, and when they dropped books off to her it was back up in the wilds of Northumberland among the tumbling remains of Hadrian's Wall. Milo loved seeing it even if he wasn't allowed off the train.

"Do you know where it is?" Milo asked.

"Not yet," Horatio said. "But I have my suspicions. There aren't many people who collect items like this. The Botanist believes the artifact has been hidden inside a book, and I'm inclined to agree. As I said, I have a theory, but I need to know for sure before I try and retrieve it."

"But how do you find out?" Milo asked.

"We may not have hard evidence of where it is yet, but we *do* know who was in possession of it last—someone who went bookwandering and was never seen again. So, if that person traveled where I think he did, we know where the poison compendium is."

"But how do we know where this person bookwandered?"

"We take a trip to the Archive." Horatio smiled.

2

Powered by Ideas

Milo's heart gave a little leap. The Archive was tied up with some of his most cherished memories. Last year, Horatio had stumbled across a map that had led them deep within layers of stories to find it, but the second time that they'd visited, Milo had accidentally ended up hiding two stowaways called Tilly and Oskar. They had been on the hunt for the Archive themselves, and he'd helped them, just a little bit, on their quest to free the bound books at the British Underlibrary. He'd never been allowed inside the Archive, but since Horatio had discovered its existence they'd been going there more and more often—so whatever Horatio was using or asking for was clearly helping his business.

"Are you listening to me?" Horatio said, clicking his fingers in front of Milo's face and snapping him out of his daydream about helping Tilly and Oskar.

"Yes," Milo said vaguely. "You want me to . . ."

"To get the Quip fired up and ready to go." Horatio sighed impatiently. "We'll need a couple more charges at least to get down to the Archive."

Horatio had never explained in detail how the Quip traveled through Story, from place to place, powered by ideas, but what Milo did know was that it could take them anywhere they could imagine. One of Milo's key jobs was keeping the engine roaring and full of the glittering *book magic* created by the ideas they collected from people as payment. It was both fuel and fee onboard the Sesquipedalian if you wanted Horatio's help to track down a book or get anywhere away from prying or official eyes. Although Milo often got the sense that there were other, even more secretive services offered, not to mention riskier methods of payment. But if he ever tried to ask Horatio, he just got one of his uncle's favorite sayings—"A conscience will lead you nowhere, boy."

"What is wrong with you today?" Horatio said, snapping Milo back into the room. "Lost in your own head! Get to it—we haven't got all day."

Milo nodded and scurried out of the dining car. He wasn't allowed in Horatio's office unchaperoned, so he scrambled up the ladder and over the top of the car, past his uncle's private quarters, before climbing back down into the engine room. It was much smaller than the engine room a usual steam train would have because there was no need for all the space to store coal. They required only enough for their reserves of *book* magic. As wood and paper were the most efficient conductors of *book magic*, they used wooden orbs to collect people's ideas and imagination, which were then burned up in the furnace to propel the train through the layers of Story.

Milo grabbed three orbs from the net full of them hanging by the door. They were giving off a faint glow, and he always got a slight tingle in his fingers when he picked them up, like a tiny static shock. He rolled them into the engine, where they started to glow more vividly as the wood caught in the flames. The Archive was tucked deep within Story, but Milo reckoned

three orbs should get them there so long as the *book magic* hadn't come from someone especially dull.

The engine cab was warm from the fire but not uncomfortably so, and Milo tucked himself into his usual corner on the floor while he kept an eye on the growing flames. Sliding a battered paperback out of the back pocket of his trousers, Milo wondered if he should stick with the more traditional way of reading or risk a spot of bookwandering before Horatio came to check on him. It was a book he visited regularly, and so he reassured himself that things were unlikely to go awry, gave the engine one last check, and then, content it would burn nicely for a while, opened the book to one of his favorite chapters and read himself inside.

> *"The mouth of the tunnel was some way from Three Chimneys, so Mother let them take their lunch with them in a basket. And the basket would do to bring the cherries back in if they found any. She also lent them her silver watch so that they should not be late for tea . . ."*

As Milo read, the tiny, warm cab started to click- clack down around him, giving way to bright sunlight, and the smell of toasted marshmallows cleared to air so fresh it almost hurt to breathe it in.

Milo was standing on the edge of a steep hill covered in trees and bushes. A few meters to his left were three children, craning their necks to see over a wooden fence: a girl who was about his age, a boy who was a year or so younger, and an even smaller girl who was up on her tiptoes in order to see better.

The hill disappeared steeply on the other side, all the way down to a train track that vanished round a corner and into the gloom of a tunnel. The children's names were Roberta (Bobbie for short), Peter, and Phyllis.

They did not know Milo, but he knew them, for he spent a great deal of his free time with the Railway Children.

3

I Always Knew
the Railway Was Enchanted

"**W**hat are you looking at?" Milo called to the three siblings, even though he knew exactly what they were looking at, having bookwandered into almost every chapter of *The Railway Children* several times over. He tucked the book back into his pocket as he walked toward them, trying not to come across as too eager.

"Hullo there," Peter said, as the three of them turned to look at Milo. "I didn't hear you behind us—you're not spying, I hope?"

"Oh, do be nice," Bobbie whispered to her brother, and smiled at Milo. "Are you from around here?" she asked politely.

"Not too far," Milo said vaguely. He didn't know the official rules, but in his experience book characters tended to be pretty good at just accepting you were there so long as you didn't do anything too strange, and Milo's worn-out trousers and shirt blended in well enough. The three siblings were so familiar to him, and it always ached a little bit that he had to reintroduce himself every time he visited them.

"Do you live nearby then?" Peter pushed. "Are you at the school?"

"No, I'm just staying with my uncle," Milo said, using his usual non-specific explanation. "But not forever, I don't think."

"Are you staying with him while your father is away, like ours?" Phyllis said. She asked it quite cheerfully, but Milo noticed that a shadow swept briefly across Bobbie's face at the mention of their father.

"My parents are dead," Milo said, as matter-of-factly as he could muster. This came up every time, and he tried to speed through it, but the three of them were always curious and wanted to talk about their own dad.

"Oh, how rotten," Peter said, his hostility immediately melting away.

"Ours is only gone away," Phyllis explained. "Although we don't know where and we're not to talk about it at home, and we're not to argue so we don't upset Mother."

Bobbie gave Milo another smile, and it was not the polite one she had offered just before but a smaller, more careful one, full of understanding.

"Anyway! We're looking for cherries!" Phyllis volunteered with a grin, wiping her hands on an already grubby apron. "There's some on the other side of the—"

She was interrupted by a rustling sort of sound. Of course

Milo knew exactly what was happening, but it was a new and strange noise to the others.

"Look!" shouted Peter, pointing at a tree on the other side of the train line. "Over there!" All four of them rushed back to the fence and saw not just one tree but several others indubitably creeping down the hill in a strange unstoppable march.

"It's moving!" Bobbie cried.

"It's magic," Phyllis said in excitement. "I always knew the railway was enchanted!"

And even Peter, who tried very hard to be desperately sensible, and Milo, who had seen it so many times before, were transfixed by the sight. The rustling noise was increasing in volume and was, in fact, now decidedly more of a *rumbling*, as trees, bushes, and rocks started to career downward. It looked like a cloth being pulled slowly off a table, bringing all the plates and glasses and food with it. Stones started to land on the train tracks, pinging and ricocheting off the metal.

"What is it?" asked Phyllis, her voice shaking a little. "It's much too magic for me. I don't like it. Let's go home."

"It's all coming down," Peter said very quietly. And then there was a pause, as if it all might stop, but it was only a breath before a scream, and all of a sudden everything started crashing down

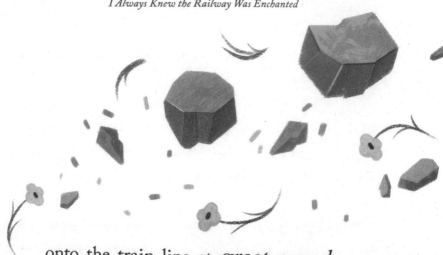

onto the train line at *great speed.*

Rocks and trees and flowers and a great deal of soil hurled downward, sending up a cloud of dust and noise.

"Look what a great mound it's made," Bobbie said, half in wonder, half in fear.

"And it's right across the train line," Milo pointed out, even though he knew Phyllis would say something similar if he didn't.

"How will they move it?" she asked instead.

"I don't know," Bobbie said helplessly.

"When does the next—" Milo started, but the awful problem had already occurred to Peter.

"The 11:29 hasn't gone by yet," Peter said, horror-struck. "We must let them know at the station, or there'll be a most frightful accident."

"Let's run then!" Bobbie said, pushing off from the fence immediately.

"But is there time?" Milo said, and Peter clapped him on the shoulder in a very stern sort of way.

"He's right," Peter said, pale-faced with responsibility. "Clever chap—it's awfully good luck you turned up when you did. There's no chance, girls—it's ten miles away and it's already past eleven." He showed them their mother's watch to prove the point.

"We can't just stand by and wait for a horrible accident to happen," Bobbie said, pink spots of anxiety on her cheeks.

"Couldn't we do something to the wires?" Phyllis suggested. "Can you climb up a telegraph pole?" she asked Milo hopefully.

"Don't be daft," Peter cut in.

"They do it in the war!" Phyllis said. "I know I've heard of it!"

"They only *cut* them, silly," Peter argued. "And that doesn't do any good."

"If only we could get the train driver's attention somehow," Milo said, earning him another appreciative clap on the shoulder from Peter.

"But with what?" Peter said. "If only we had something red for danger."

"And how?" Phyllis pointed out. "For even if we had something to wave, the train wouldn't see us till it got round the corner, and . . ."

"But we must wave anyway," Bobbie said desperately. "And we must *run!*"

4

Knowing the Answer in Advance

The four of them clambered down the rough wooden steps set into the hillside and picked their way over to the huge mound of debris on the railway line. Bobbie gave a great sigh as they edged past it—it was even more intimidatingly large now they were down next to it.

"It will all work out okay, I'm sure of it," Milo reassured her, and she smiled at him warmly.

"I do hope so," she said. "I just . . . Oh, I just don't think the train will see us in time between coming out of the tunnel and turning the corner. There's just not enough time to slow down. And it will be so horrible, and it will all be our fault that we didn't think of a better plan in time!"

Now, Milo had read *The Railway Children* and he knew exactly what plan they would come up with if left to their own devices. Every once in a while, he couldn't resist being the one to solve the puzzle, with the rather substantial benefit of knowing the answer in advance. But it is not good form to claim an idea that isn't yours, and always made Milo feel a bit unpleasant in his stomach afterward, and so he waited for Phyllis.

"Oh, how hot I am!" she started to complain, her face red and worried. "I thought it was going to be cold; I wish we hadn't put on our . . ." And there she paused as the idea struck her. "Our flannel petticoats!"

Bobbie turned to look at her, relief in her face. "Oh, Phyllis!" she said. "Yes! They're red! Let's take them off!"

The first time that Milo had visited this bit of the book he had been a little alarmed, and not quite sure exactly which part of the girls' old-fashioned outfits was the petticoat. But it was simply one layer of many under their dresses, and they easily and quickly slid their red petticoats down and stepped out of them with very little fuss. Phyllis was a little nervous about ruining their clothes, but Bobbie and Peter quickly set to it, ripping the sturdy waistbands off and then tearing each petticoat into three ragged squares.

"This is very important," Milo explained to Phyllis as they watched Peter try to wrestle some saplings into submission with a very blunt penknife in order to make flagpoles to hang the torn red petticoats from. "There'd be a really bad accident if the train crashed into the pile of rocks, and you won't get into any trouble at all—you're . . . we're saving lots of people's lives by doing this, I promise. It's worth ruining your petticoats for, and your mother will agree."

Phyllis nodded her head, determined, and the two of them joined Bobbie and Peter in threading the saplings through the two rough holes Peter had just about managed to carve in the thick flannel material.

"You look awfully happy," Peter said, looking up at Milo, red-faced and worried. "I say, you do know that it'll be a terrible thing to see if we can't attract the train driver's attention."

"I'm sorry," Milo said, caught out in his enthusiasm for being part of their team. "I'm not happy at the thought of the accident, I swear. It's just . . . Well, it's great to all work together, isn't it?"

"I suppose," Peter said, still a little suspiciously, and then Milo heard Bobbie whisper to him as they turned back to the flags.

"*Don't*, Peter," Bobbie was saying quietly. "Haven't you ever had that feeling when you're in trouble and all you want to do is laugh from the horribleness of it all? I think perhaps it is something like that that the poor boy's feeling, and we shouldn't judge anyone for how they are under pressure like this. I feel quite light-headed, for one, and you've become even sterner than usual."

Milo pretended he hadn't heard.

"How about we make some piles of the stones," he suggested, wanting to prove himself to Peter. "And stick two of the flags on either side of the track, and then we hold one each?"

"Right, yes," Peter said, appeased. "Good plan. Although

I should have thought I should have two, as it was my idea to wave something red."

"But they're our petticoats!" Phyllis argued, as the four of them gathered as many loose stones and rocks as they could to wedge the flags into.

"And it was Phyllis and Bobbie who thought of them," Milo pointed out.

"Oh, shush, all of you," Bobbie said. "There are four flags and four of us, and we mustn't argue. Peter, you can have mine if you really feel you must have two."

"It doesn't matter," he said. "I was just saying."

And then there was a horrible pause as they stood ready, flags in hand, worrying that perhaps the train had already gone past and they should have run for the station instead—but then there it was.

The tracks started to murmur, there was a screech of a whistle, and the plume of white steam came into view.

"Stand firm," Peter shouted. "And wave like mad!"

5

The End of a Book
Is a Dangerous Place

The line of white steam was getting closer and closer, and the tracks were humming as the train approached.

"They don't see us! They won't see us! It's all no good!" Bobbie shouted, standing right on the train tracks, waving her flag wildly from side to side. The juddering of the tracks was making their piles of stones wobble, and Bobbie leaned over and grabbed one of the toppling flags before it fell out of sight completely.

"Keep off the line!" Peter yelled, holding Phyllis's arm tight to stop her joining their sister.

"Not yet! Not yet!" Bobbie shouted, waving and waving. The train itself was in view now, huge and black and roaring toward them.

"Go and get her!" Peter yelled to Milo. "I need to keep hold of Phyllis!"

"No!" Milo shouted back over the din. "She knows what she's doing!" And he ran and joined her right on the track, waving his flag as tall and as wide as he could, the gigantic front of the train barreling toward them. He had seen this from every possible angle on his various bookwandering visits; he'd held Phyllis while Peter had grabbed Bobbie, he'd stood with Bobbie, and sometimes he didn't even speak to the children and just watched it all unfold from the top of the hill.

But this moment, just as the train approached, never got less frightening. And Milo could hear his uncle's voice in his head, telling him that being run over by a train in a book was going to cause you just as much damage as in real life. And then, just as it seemed too late, right as Milo thought they had miscalculated and his presence had thrown the whole story off-kilter, there was the scream of a brake, and the train started to slow down.

Milo grabbed Bobbie's arm and pulled her to the side as the great steam train slowed, miraculously quickly for the bulk of it, and stopped just in time. Bobbie was still waving her flags weakly, and once the train had come to a complete stop, she fainted onto the grass.

The engine driver clambered down from the cab, sweating profusely and breathing heavily. Milo felt the weight of his gaze as the driver sized up the situation and the four children, and Milo hoped with his whole heart that he took them for siblings. His brown skin had occasionally caused problems when he was bookwandering, especially in stories that had been published a long time ago. Even though the magic of bookwandering helped anyone blend into any book, he sometimes felt the sharp edge of people's stares before the story magic kicked in and smoothed everything out.

"Goodness," the driver said. "That was a very close thing, weren't it? Aye, it doesn't bear thinking about what might have happened if the four of you hadn't had your wits about you. You brothers and sisters then?"

"More or less," Peter said, nodding at Milo.

And there it was. Why Milo returned again and again to this book. Because when it came down to it, whichever bit of the story he bookwandered into—whether the plot stuck closely to what E. Nesbit had written way back in 1905 or whether Milo changed its course a little—Bobbie, Peter, and Phyllis always claimed him as their own.

There was much to talk about, but the immediate concern was, of course, Bobbie—who was still lying unconscious on the grass, her lips worryingly blue. The driver picked her up gently and edged his way up the steps into the first-class carriage, settling her down on a luxurious velvet seat. He told the others to watch over her—as though they would do anything else.

"I'll just 'ave a look at this 'ere mound of yours, and then we'll run you back to the station and get her seen to," he said in a broad Yorkshire accent. Ten minutes later the train started heading backward toward the station it had just come through.

"I believe that's what people look like when they're dead," Phyllis said very quietly over Milo's shoulder as the train reversed carefully.

"Don't," Peter said, and Phyllis looked as though she might burst into tears.

"She's not dead," Milo said calmly. "Definitely not. Look, if you put your hand over her mouth, you can feel her breath. She's just fainted from the stress of it all."

And just as Phyllis was reaching out to feel her sister's breath, Bobbie rolled over and started crying. It wasn't long before Peter and Phyllis were poking fun at her for fainting, the teasing a comfortable cover for their affection. As usual, Milo felt the urge to join in, but sometimes it is just not possible to tease someone for fainting, or laugh at them, unless you are their brother or sister. Not to mention that you should never poke fun at someone unless you would be happy for the tables to be turned, and for them to laugh at you, and that you would know without question that it was full of familiarity and deep-in-the-bones love.

Before long, they could feel the train slowing down as it carefully drew into and stopped at the station, and the driver came back to find them.

"It's a bit of a to-do and no mistake," he said. "I'm glad it won't be up to me to clear that mound, but, goodness me, it's a good job the four of you saw it and waved those red . . ."

"Petticoats," Phyllis supplied, waving hers enthusiastically to demonstrate. "Red flannel petticoats."

"I see," the driver said, a little awkwardly. "Well, if red flannel petticoats were what stopped the train in time, then you won't catch me saying that they weren't the best tool for the task in hand. Now, let's get you down and inside. Looks like you might need a sweet cup of tea, miss," he said to Bobbie. "And I think there's probably a lot of people that will want to thank you."

He helped Bobbie climb down onto the station platform, and Peter and Phyllis followed behind. But Milo stayed sitting on the soft blue cushions and watched from the window as they were met with applause by the station staff. He pulled the book out of his pocket and flicked to the last page to read himself out.

"At the end of the field, among the thin gold spikes of grass and the harebells and Gypsy roses and St. John's Wort, we may just take one last look, over our shoulders, at the white house where neither we nor anyone else is wanted now."

Within seconds he was sitting back in the hot, stuffy engine car of the Quip, by himself. However many adventures he had with the Railway Children, Milo could never go as far as he wanted. The end of a book was a dangerous place, and you risked tumbling into the Endpapers if you lingered too long. And even if it were safe to stay so long, the narrator did not follow the children into their last scene of the book but watched from outside. If you strayed beyond what was on the page, the results were unpredictable.

Stories could warp or break or vanish; scenes became shadows of themselves.

The family did not want for anything else as they had each other, and although it broke his heart to watch with the narrator from outside, Milo knew the idea that he held in his imagination had to be enough.

6

A Slice of Imagination

The only time Milo had ever truly felt part of a team was when Tilly and Oskar had been onboard the Quip. He wished he could bookwander into his own memories and relive it again and again. They'd appeared seemingly out of nowhere on the way to the Archive, and the hour the three of them had spent pulling together bits of information to make a plan was one of Milo's happiest memories. He had actually been useful; he had known things that helped them; he hadn't just tagged along or kept out of sight.

But, of course, even that had been tainted. Milo's uncle had a habit of extracting favors from people he thought might prove to be useful, and once he'd realized that Tilly had unusual bookwandering abilities, he'd made sure to get the promise of a favor from her. It soured everything, even though Milo knew that Horatio calling it in was probably the only way he would ever get to see Tilly or Oskar again.

"Milo!" came his uncle's shout, and Milo shoved the book away, relieved he'd left just in time. "We're nearly there. Get ready!"

Milo jumped up and pulled hard on the brake lever to slow the train. The Quip did not run on tracks of iron, and so the squeal was imaginary—not that it made it any quieter.

As the train slowed, the sparkling darkness of Story started to knit together into something more solid. Horatio wouldn't talk about how the Quip worked, saying he was wary of anyone finding out its mysteries. Sometimes Milo did wonder if Horatio even knew the answer himself.

"Who would I tell?" Milo would always argue, whenever his uncle refused to talk about the Quip's magic. "You don't let me talk to anyone!"

"It's just easier this way," Horatio would reply shortly. "I have no doubt you already told Matilda and Oskar everything you do know and would have given away all our secrets if you'd known them."

And he was not wrong. For now, Milo was curious but content; he didn't know everything—or even much—about the Quip, but it was enough for the time being. Milo loved how it slid through layers of Story like a hot knife through butter (unless it had to swerve round an unexpected plot twist). The deeper within Story they were, the more the landscape bent to allow for a train; everything was malleable, and if you could imagine it, it could come into being. When they took the train outside the realms of stories, it had to scrape out a slice of imagination to catch on to, but places like the Archive simply allowed the Quip in and re-formed around it. So now, when they pulled up to the platform, it was at a traditional train station as if there were regular services stopping there.

The best bit about visiting the Archive was that Milo was allowed off the train. He'd never actually been inside before, but, as the woman who looked after it had already met him because of Tilly and Oskar, Horatio begrudgingly didn't make him stay hidden. Milo waited, as usual, to see if there was anything that his uncle needed him to offload or any papers to get ready, but today was different, and Horatio beckoned with a crooked finger.

"You're coming too," he said. Terrified of saying anything that might make his uncle change his mind, Milo simply nodded and followed.

"It's even worse than last time," Horatio said as they walked across the platform. He was right. Every time they had arrived at the Archive, it was slightly more bedraggled. The previously neat cobblestones were cracked and dirty, with moss and weeds poking through. Loose trails of ivy hung on the crumbling red brick walls, and the ornate golden gate that led to the Archive itself was only hanging by its hinges on one side, rusty and creaking.

"Good grief," Horatio muttered under his breath as they passed through the gate and saw an even more unsettling sight.

Among dead and gray gardens and blackened trees, what had been a very grand building was now just barely standing. A central block was still clinging on, but the wings were little more than piles of brick and glass. "Things have obviously deteriorated," Horatio said, although he sounded more curious than upset.

"Is Artemis expecting us?" Milo said, risking a question, hoping he'd get a chance to talk to the friendly woman who had helped Tilly and Oskar.

"Not this visit," Horatio said. "I didn't have time to let her know, but I'm sure that she'll be more than willing to help. If she still can, that is, given the state of things here. Now hurry up, and no more questions."

The two of them approached a set of steps that, like everything else, was cracked and broken. They picked their way over the loose stones, and Horatio went to pull the extravagant but moth-eaten velvet bell rope—which promptly came off in his hand.

He dropped it on the ground in disgust and knocked firmly on the peeling paintwork of the door instead.

7

The World's Imagination

A few moments later the door swung open to show a woman dressed in black. Milo tried not to stare, though he couldn't help but notice that the edges of her skirts were frayed and that there was a rip in the sleeve of her shirt. Her hair was perfectly pinned, however, and she wore a calm, warm smile.

"Artemis," Horatio said.

"Welcome," the woman said graciously. "It's good to see you again, Horatio, and I believe this must be your nephew. Milo, we've never had the pleasure of being formally introduced, although of course I have caught glimpses of you in the past. My name is Artemis. Welcome to the Archive. I can only apologize that things are so . . . cluttered."

"Hi," Milo said, shaking the hand Artemis was holding out and thinking that "cluttered" was an extremely understated way of describing the situation. "Thanks for having me."

"So polite." Artemis smiled.

"Not usually," Horatio said, which Milo did not think was fair, all things considered.

"Now, how can I help?" Artemis said. "I don't believe you made an appointment, otherwise I would have tidied up."

"No, I'm sorry to drop in on you," Horatio said, not sounding especially apologetic. "But, with all due respect, I'm not sure more warning would have helped with the . . . tidying up."

Milo thought he saw a flash of irritation sweep across Artemis's face, but an instant later she was smiling calmly again, and he wondered if he'd been mistaken.

"Only some surface damage, I assure you," she said. "I have a lot on my plate at the moment; as you know, our Archivists have quite recently left."

"They saw what happened to Mr. Shakespeare?" Horatio said.

"They did," she said. "I am sure you know all about this, Milo?"

"I met Will, yes," he said. "He came to London with us on the Quip and helped Tilly stop all the *book magic* from being stolen."

"Well, sadly, many of his colleagues, other very distinguished writers, have followed his course," Artemis explained, "and decided not to remain here to try and rebuild this place as a refuge for bookwanderers but instead to disintegrate into Story, to become part of the world's imagination and not linger in a physical form. They've chosen to let their stories live on in their place, leaving me to deal with all of this on my own."

"So how many Archivists are left here now?" Horatio asked.

"Well, to be precise . . . none," Artemis said.

"None at all?"

"It is just me here now," she repeated.

"But . . . and again, with all due respect, are you able to continue here without any of the Archivists? Will new Archivists come? Is that not the purpose of this place?" Horatio pushed.

"The purpose of this place has evolved over the centuries," Artemis said. "The Archivists did not create this place, but rather . . . bookwanderers did. Daring thinkers and experimenters in *book magic* made its walls, and then the great writers were drawn here by those huge supplies of *book magic*."

"Can you get new ones?" Milo asked politely. "There's still a lot of good writers alive, so I suppose they'll . . . you know, die at some point, and then they could come here and help you."

"I am not sure that we are holding on to enough *book magic* to get them here anymore," Artemis said. "The thing is—"

"He doesn't need to know all this," Horatio cut in.

"Would you like to know?" Artemis asked Milo directly. He looked between her and Horatio's stern face and cautiously nodded. Horatio sighed and shrugged.

"Keep it quick," he said. "Stories cost time, and we're on a schedule."

Artemis raised an eyebrow for Milo's benefit, and Milo had the lurch in his stomach he always felt when someone invited him to be part of anything: a team, a plan, even a joke at his uncle's expense was enough to draw him to that person, like an ever-hopeful moth to a friendly flame.

"Well, to keep it brief to appease your uncle," Artemis said with a warm smile, "you've got the general gist. The Archive was created as a haven and an escape for bookwanderers—somewhere to come and marvel at the magic of stories and see what they could do. And because of the huge well of *book magic* that created the place, for generations and generations, writers who have contributed a particularly notable amount to the collective imagination have been pulled to the Archive after they died. In past years, the Archive has helped bookwanderers, guided them or even just passed time with those who followed the maps that showed them the way here. And you saw how Will was able to help your friends Tilly and Oskar . . . Have you kept in touch?"

Milo shook his head, embarrassed to admit that even though they'd promised to write, he hadn't heard anything at all from them, and Artemis describing them as friends made him feel like he'd been caught in a lie.

"Well, it must be tricky to keep in touch with someone onboard something as clever as the Quip," Artemis said reassuringly. "Anyway, the point is that it was pure *book magic* that created and maintained the Archive and drew its former residents here, and well . . . you see the state we're in. I don't think we will be troubled by new guests."

"But what will you do?" Milo asked, worried.

"While undeniably the Archivists themselves were a huge part of this place," she said, "there is still the Archive itself."

"Isn't this building the Archive?"

"We call it that, but the whole place is named for one specific hall," she said. "Part of why it existed in the first place, before the Archivists started being pulled here. Would you like to see?"

"That won't be necessary," Horatio interjected. "But it is why *I* have come. I need to find out where a particular individual has been bookwandering."

"You know that I am not permitted to show you the Records of other bookwanderers, Mr. Bolt," Artemis said.

Horatio rolled his eyes. "There's no need to put on airs and graces in front of the boy," he said. "I think the time has passed for keeping up appearances, considering your general situation here . . ."

Again, that flash of irritation swept across Artemis's face and passed in the fraction of a second.

She inclined her head slightly. "Very well," she said. "Who are you trying to find?"

8

Adventures Never Happen to People Who Sit Still and Follow the Rules

Horatio took Artemis by the elbow and hurried her ahead.

"Can the boy stay behind?" Horatio asked.

"I don't think it's safe," Artemis said. "As you pointed out yourself, the building is no longer very sturdy."

"Fine." Horatio shrugged and looked over his shoulder at Milo. "Don't even think about eavesdropping on our conversation," he barked. "Artemis has said you can see the Archive, but you're to stay by the entrance and not poke your nose anywhere it's not wanted—understood?"

"Yes," Milo said, happy to agree to anything that would let him see this mysterious archive—and indeed anything that would allow him to be a bigger part of whatever his uncle was up to. He walked a few paces behind the adults, and as it was very quiet, he thought that perhaps if he accidentally overheard the name of the person his uncle was looking for, he couldn't be blamed—how would Horatio even know? There was no one to tell. But they were talking too quietly for him to pick anything up, and he couldn't get any closer without risking his uncle realizing he was listening, so he had to content himself with soaking up being off the train for once, even if it was in this eerie, crumbling building.

It did not take long for the three of them to reach the end of a corridor, where a pair of slightly grubby white doors stood, one of them slightly ajar. Artemis pushed it further open with a creak that made Milo's skin crawl and gestured for them both to follow her. Inside was a huge hall that clearly used to be very grand, and presumably much cleaner. There were no windows in its white-painted, cracked walls, although the high ceilings had huge holes in them that you could see the sky through. The hall was full of shelves and shelves, all packed full of white books of various widths, with more piles of books on the floor, many of them haphazardly lying open.

It was obvious from Horatio's reaction that things had deteriorated in here as well.

"You can still find everyone's Record?" he asked bluntly.

"Yes, of course," Artemis said, as though this was a strange question, despite the mess. "Those books aren't shelved purely because I have been in the middle of doing some research."

"Is that what these Records are for?" Horatio said. "Your personal research?"

"Mr. Bolt, may I remind you while we have come to a mutually beneficial arrangement over access to some of the Archive's resources, that does not mean it is appropriate for you to question the way I take care of this place, or what I spend my time doing when you are not here. I was appointed Bibliognost, and how I fulfill that role is no concern of yours. If you do not find the way it is run satisfactory, you are welcome to do your research elsewhere, and I wish you the best of luck finding the information you seek."

"Noted," Horatio said begrudgingly, turning back to Milo. "Now, you, boy, what did I say about eavesdropping?" He gestured to a low white wooden bench by the door. "Sit there and don't touch anything. If I call for you, come straightaway. Understood?"

Milo nodded, again, and sat on the uncomfortable bench. Horatio and Artemis walked through the shelves, picking their way over fallen books, torn pages, and parts of the wooden floor that were splintered and lifting up in scratchy points.

Milo tapped his fingers on the edge of the bench, crossed and uncrossed his legs to stave off pins and needles, and tried his best to make out anything interesting from where he was sitting. But everything was just white, or had been, and the dirt and disarray made it hard to read what was on the spines of the books. The problem was that if you put a curious person, especially a curious child, in a mysterious and magical place and tell them to stay still, your chances of success are slim. And Milo had read enough books to know that adventures never happen to people who sit still and follow the rules.

He could no longer see or hear the two adults, and so he tentatively stood up and tested how quiet he could be. The worn soles of his boots barely made any sound on the wooden floors, and he very slowly crept toward the nearest bookcase. All the spines of the books were marked with names, in alphabetical order by surname, like in a library. As someone who lived and worked alongside books, Milo knew the risk of trying to slide one volume off a shelf packed with heavy tomes: he'd been a victim of the domino effect too many times before. Instead, he picked up one of the open books that was lying on the floor and tilted it to see what was printed on the spine.

The name, embossed in peeling gold, was Esme Bowman. The very first page was a neat list of information about her. She was born in 1946 and had died only a year or so ago. She had lived most of her life in Hokitika, New Zealand, and was registered as a bookwanderer at the New Zealand Underlibrary in Wellington. Milo flicked through the pages and realized this was a record of everywhere Esme had bookwandered, from when she first found out she could do it, when she was nine, right up until the last time, when she'd traveled into a book of poems written by someone called Mary Oliver. Milo wondered what it would be like to bookwander into poetry and made a mental note to try it. Most of the Record was transcribed in a very formal style, describing the books Esme went into and an overview of what happened there. One of the last entries said:

> *"Esme bookwandered into Chapter 23 of Persuasion by Jane Austen and observed the events. She returned again to the same scene shortly afterward and spoke with Captain Wentworth."*

There was a whole life contained in its pages. Milo picked up another book, this one much slimmer, as the bookwanderer was still only twelve, the same age as him. But he nearly dropped it when, on turning to the last few pages, he realized it was still being written. An invisible pen was writing on the pages, describing someone—Milo checked the spine: Zebulun Barker—bookwandering right at that point inside a book called *The Girl of Ink and Stars*.

Milo scanned the Records and saw names in all different languages and, when he cracked the books open, saw that their contents were all written in those same languages. He looked about in wonder, surrounded by the lives of so many bookwanderers from so many places and times.

"I suppose I have one in here somewhere too," he said under his breath. "And Horatio and Tilly and Oskar. I wonder if I can find them."

Although many of the books on the floor were out of order, a glance told him he was definitely in the "B" section, which meant his own Record was most likely the nearest. "Probably safest," he mused. It was one thing looking at a stranger's Record, but looking at Tilly's would feel like reading her diary, he thought. He knew that he wouldn't want anyone to know how many times he visited the railway children.

Trailing his fingertips along the spines of the Records, he followed the alphabet through Baker and Bentham and Birch, and then, just after Boggi, he saw Bolt. His breath caught a little, because of course, right there on the shelves, were the Records of his parents. Two white books with "Saira Bolt" and "Asher Bolt" stamped on the sides. Milo suddenly felt a little dizzy when he realized there might be even more family members here for him to discover. His rush of excitement was quickly replaced by disappointment so sharp he could almost taste it, for the only other Bolt on the shelf was Horatio.

"Hang on," he said. Even if there were no other members of the Bolt family who were bookwanderers, there should have been one more: his. But after Asher, Horatio, and Saira Bolt, instead of a white book, there was something else. Something completely out of place. There was no official Record, only a tattered leather scrapbook, bound together with a leather cord.

Milo pulled it off the shelf and stared at it. Written on the front, not embossed with gold but

scrawled

in

black

ink,

was

his

own

n a m e .

9

A Small Detour

The book, if it could be called a book, was made from roughly cut, thick paper, and Milo could see that in between its pages were tucked other loose sheets of different sizes—but before he had chance to look properly, he heard the footsteps of his uncle and Artemis returning.

Panicking, Milo shoved the book down the back of his trousers, under his jumper. He ran as quickly and quietly as he could back to the bench and sat down carefully, making sure the bulk of the book was pressed against the wall. As soon as he sat down, he wished he'd tried to take his parents' Records too, or even instead of whatever *this* was. He told himself off for getting distracted by his own strange Record; what if this was the universe providing him with this one opportunity to find out what happened to his parents, and he'd wasted it because he was selfish?

"Milo!" his uncle shouted.

"Yes!" he called, trying to sound casual and a little bored, as though he had been sitting on his own with nothing to do for half an hour, even though his heart was hammering hard inside his chest. "Do you need me?"

"Just checking you're where you're supposed to be," Horatio said, coming into view between the bookshelves. He was holding one of the white books under his arm, and Artemis was just behind him, looking distressed. "But I do have a couple of questions for you. So, that girl Matilda?" Horatio said. "I know she wasn't especially exciting as a conversationalist, but you did spend an hour or so with her."

"Uh . . . yes, I remember," Milo said, utterly bemused by the fact that his uncle hadn't realized how important that day was to him. "Her and her best friend, Oskar."

"Yes, them," Horatio said. "You spoke to them a bit when I wasn't there, yes? No doubt telling them far more than you should have."

"Yes," Milo agreed. "That is, yes, I spoke to them, but I didn't . . ." He tailed off and blushed.

"Never mind that for now— it's why I don't tell you anything important," Horatio said. "And do you remember that Matilda had some unusual abilities?"

"Yes," Milo said, more slowly, still amazed that his uncle thought it a possibility that he might have forgotten any detail at all of that brilliant day.

"Did she tell you anything else about those abilities?" Horatio asked.

"Um, I'm not sure," Milo said tentatively. "Why?"

"She owes me a favor," Horatio said. "And it's time to call it in."

"Milo," Artemis said, more gently than Horatio. "It would be extremely helpful—for your uncle—if you could remember anything else Tilly might have told you about her book-wandering powers."

"She can . . . well, she can bring things out of books, can't she?" Milo said, knowing that Tilly had said that in front of Horatio, and so he hopefully wasn't causing more problems for her than Horatio was already going to create.

"She didn't say anything else?" Horatio asked again.

Milo shook his head and shrugged. The thing was that Milo truly didn't know anything else. When Tilly had talked vaguely about her bookwandering working differently because she was half fictional, he hadn't pushed her for more details. She'd implied there was more than she was sharing, but he wasn't the sort of person to try and get people to reveal more about themselves than they wanted to, and he'd seen that Tilly was the same. Neither she nor Oskar had tried to get more out of Milo when he'd given them a short version of how he'd come to end up living on the Quip. It was part of why that day was so special: he'd felt understood.

"What a waste of time bringing you," Horatio said. "Remind me not to bother again."

"Oh, come now," Artemis said. "It's good for Milo to see a

bit more of what you do. Why, don't you want him to take over the family business in the future?"

"No," Horatio said shortly, looking up at Artemis sharply. "Why would you say that?"

"Just a question," Artemis said.

"Milo isn't interested in taking over the Quip," Horatio said, so slowly and clearly that it made Milo glance around, as if there were someone else listening in. Horatio shook his head and forced a laugh. "Anyway, Milo would have to prove he's worthy of it, and he's not done much to provide hope yet."

"I see," Artemis said. "And how do you feel about that, Milo?"

"It doesn't matter how he feels," Horatio said.

Milo just looked at the floor, desperately trying not to cry in front of Artemis. He was used to these sorts of comments from his uncle, but that didn't mean they didn't have any impact, even if it was more like picking at a scab rather than scratching a fresh wound.

"It doesn't make much difference to the plan anyway," Horatio went on. "We'll just have to go and find Tilly, and we'll take it from there."

"What do you need her to do?" Milo asked nervously.

"Considering I already told you about the compendium we're looking for, I don't see the harm in telling you that we need her help to retrieve it," Horatio said. He held out the Record he was carrying. "Someone, somehow, has tampered with this Record, and it's not showing its contents to any old reader." Horatio flicked through the pages, and Milo could see that they were completely blank, aside from the information about the bookwanderer on the very first page. "But that's no bother," Horatio continued. "It just means a small detour. And once I know exactly where this bookwanderer was last seen I'll know where the poison compendium is, and once I know where it is I'll need Matilda to get it out again."

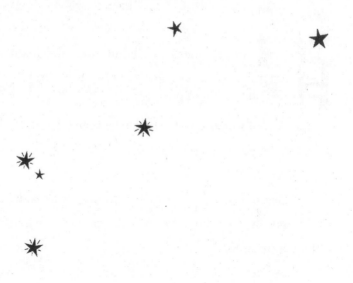

10

Considerably More Questions

Horatio strode ahead, with no time for politeness for Artemis now he had got what he came for.

"Try not to take what your uncle says to heart too much," Artemis said quietly to Milo. "He's only . . . Well, I think he's only trying to keep you . . . safe."

"Safe?" Milo said in surprise. "From what? Having friends?"

"I'm sure he has his reasons for whatever he is doing," was all Artemis said. "But you must take care of yourself as well, Milo. Pay attention."

"To what?"

"Just pay attention," she said. "Your uncle . . . He has irons in many fires and is trying to do very many things at once, including looking after you. I think he loves you, even if he is not very good at showing it."

The word "love" made Milo stop in his tracks; it was not a word he'd heard used much, and Horatio had certainly never told him that he loved him. It made him feel strange all over just thinking about it.

"Anyway, I'm used to him now," Milo said, shaking himself out of the moment, trying to sound as though he didn't really care that much. "I'd rather be on the Quip than back with the Marters, and that's the choice I've got."

"They're people who looked after you after your parents died?"

Milo was momentarily surprised that she would know this, but he supposed that she had access to a great deal of information about bookwanderers. He nodded. "Speaking of which," he said, Artemis's friendliness encouraging him. "Would you cover for . . . I mean, would you mind if I just ran back and quickly checked something? I'd be so fast that he wouldn't notice, I promise."

"To check your parents' Records, I assume? I would have thought you'd have looked while you were waiting," she said, and he blushed, but she waved his embarrassment away. "It's what I would have done. But I'm afraid not. Firstly, there's really no way we could do it before your uncle noticed, and secondly it's strictly prohibited."

"But Horatio is taking someone else's with him!" Milo said in frustration. "How is he allowed but not me?"

"Yes, he is," Artemis said. "But . . . Well, I have given him permission in exchange for . . . Which is to say . . . we have come to an arrangement. These Records are my responsibility, but I take each of his requests on a case-by-case basis, and it depends on whose he is wanting to look at and . . . anyway," she stopped. "You do not need to worry about it."

"So, is it you who writes in those books?" Milo asked. "Is it you who made it harder for him to find out what he wants— have you made that Record blank?"

"No," she explained. "I don't write the books, and I can't change or mask what is in them—they're fueled purely by *book magic* and created and honed by the people who first built this place. The Records track the *book magic* that all bookwanderers have in them, the magic they use to travel into books, which leaves a trace behind. I'm not sure if you've spent enough time in Underlibraries, but it's a more intense version of something they call stamping—when Underlibrarians use *book magic* to follow someone through books. I have very little control over the contents of the Records—none, really—but it's worth remembering, Milo, that we leave a trace wherever we go, whether it's in the world, or in stories."

"So, it kind of seems like it's quite hard to, sort of, keep on top of things, on your own?" he asked politely, and Artemis raised an eyebrow at him.

"It would be foolish of me to lie and say otherwise," she admitted. "But, Milo, the truth is that without the Archive, I am not sure who I am or where I can go. I am not a human, as you are. I am not entirely certain how I came to be—I believe I was written into existence, or something similar, purely to care for this place and preserve its magic. And I've failed, in that and in so many other things. I should perhaps feel at peace with this all coming to an end, but there is something that will not allow me to let go. But this is a lot to burden you with. I am sorry. As you may have realized, I do not have many people to talk to, and even fewer that I trust."

"I don't mind," Milo said simply. "It's nice to talk to someone."

"Well, so long as I am here, you are always welcome to visit and to talk," Artemis said. "I would love to hear about how you get on with Tilly—you must be excited to see her again."

"Yes . . . Although I don't want her to get into danger because of what my uncle is going to ask her to do."

"Perhaps you should make sure you go with them," Artemis suggested. "And then you can both come and tell me all about it."

"If you knew that I lived with the Marters for a bit," Milo started, feeling the book tucked into his waistband, pushing against his back, "does that mean you know about what happened to my family?"

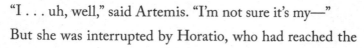

"In what sense?" Artemis asked carefully.

"I don't know anything about any of them," Milo said. "I only know Horatio. And I did look on the shelves, but I only found my parents' Records, and I don't even know what name to look under for anyone else."

"I . . . uh, well," said Artemis. "I'm not sure it's my—"

But she was interrupted by Horatio, who had reached the

main hall. He paused, as if it had just occurred to him that Milo and Artemis could have been talking about anything at all.

"I've got what I came for," he said sharply. "Enough chitter-chattering. We need to find this chap and get the book from him. Ms. Artemis, a pleasure, and always interesting to see what you're . . . working on."

"I hope you find what you're looking for," she said.

Horatio only smirked and stalked down the steps into the dead garden.

"It was nice to meet you," Milo said to Artemis as he followed.

"You too, Milo," Artemis said. "Take good care of what you've borrowed."

"I haven't . . ." He stopped. "You know I took it? I wasn't stealing—I promise—it's just that it was different from all the others, and . . ."

"It's all right," Artemis said. "But promise you'll bring it back? When you visit with Tilly, perhaps?"

"I'll try," Milo said. "But I don't get a lot of say in where we go."

"For now." Artemis smiled.

And with that she closed the door of the Archive behind her, leaving Milo standing outside the crumbling building with considerably more questions than he'd arrived with.

11

It's Not All Magic and Whimsy

Horatio was waiting impatiently for him on the train platform.

"What did she say to you?" he asked.

"Nothing," Milo said.

"Don't say what you don't mean," Horatio said.

"Not nothing," Milo tried again. "But she was just chatting, about nothing important, I meant. I was asking her about the white books."

"Trying to get information out of her, I suppose? What you don't know can't hurt you."

"I was just curious," Milo said. "Anyway, why is information bad?"

"It isn't, but it's valuable, and keeping track of who is in possession of what knowledge is vital to my work. I don't want anyone knowing my business without my say-so, understood?" Horatio said curtly.

"I guess," Milo said. "But people have to know about the Quip, otherwise they can't hire you to find stuff for them."

"That does not mean they need to know how it works, who works onboard, or who my other clients are," Horatio said. "There are people in this world who . . . I am not the only person who is interested in knowledge and leverage, and you may not believe it, but there are people who are willing to go to far more extreme lengths than I to get it. I see the way you look at me, Milo. You think I have no conscience, but I assure you there's a reason for everything I do and that there are worse things than living here with me."

"I know," Milo said, "I wouldn't want to go back to the Marters."

"I'm not talking about them," Horatio said darkly. "I am fairly confident of where I'll need to go with Matilda to get this compendium for the Botanist, and it's not a safe place. It's somewhere illicit, and dangerous things are traded and stored, and I won't want to be caught there. There are darker forces at work in the bookwandering world than you realize—it's not all magic and whimsy."

"Is all of that to do with what happened to my parents?" Milo tried. "Were they caught up in the dark forces? Did they do something bad?"

Horatio whirled round. "What do you mean?" he demanded. "What have you heard?"

"Nothing!" Milo said, panicked by his uncle's tone. "I just

meant that you said that they died, and I don't know anything about who the rest of our family are, and so, when you mentioned dark and scary stuff, I just wondered . . ."

"Well, stop wondering. I've told you far too much, clearly."

"But I don't know who I *am*," Milo finished desperately. "How am I supposed to know who I am if I don't know where I've come from or who my parents were or what they were like?"

"If you speak in clichés, don't expect serious answers from me," Horatio said. "We carve out our own identities. What's come before has nothing to do with it. Now, that's the end of this conversation if you know what's good for you." And with that, Horatio opened the door to the carriage that served as his office and climbed up.

I could never keep so many secrets, Milo thought to himself. *I wouldn't be able to keep track.* And he presumed that was why his uncle would never let him inherit the Quip.

Horatio had left the door open, which meant he wanted Milo to follow. Milo felt the bulk of the stolen scrapbook warm against his back, and he hurriedly pulled it out, yanked open the engine carriage door, and slid it onto the floor, trusting that he would have a chance to retrieve it long before Horatio ventured into the hot, stuffy cab. He smoothed his jumper down and followed Horatio into his office, where his uncle had sat down at his wide wooden desk, the white Record lying closed in front of him.

"As there's something stopping me from seeing where this man, one Theodore Grant, is bookwandering, I'm going to have to go inside his Record and see what I can find."

"You're going to bookwander *into* a Record? Is that allowed?"

Horatio just raised an eyebrow in response. He did not care whether things were allowed.

"But would it work?" Milo asked instead.

"Yes," Horatio answered confidently.

"But what would it be like inside?" Milo asked. "If it's blank, like this one is?"

"I can't say I have any idea what the inside of a Record looks like, blank or otherwise," his uncle said shortly. "Usually the information is right there for the picking. I can't imagine it's so much different from any other book. I've bookwandered into all sorts before and never . . . rarely encountered anything that caused any real problems. And once I'm sure exactly where this Theodore is hiding, we can be off to London to call in that favor from Matilda. Hopefully I should only be gone for a few minutes."

"Don't you want Artemis to go with you?" Milo said. "Mightn't she know how to do it properly?"

"Artemis may know a great deal about these Records, but remember that she isn't a bookwanderer," Horatio said. "There's also no reason to share more than necessary with her about what I'm looking for or where I'm headed next. Remember what I said about not sharing more than we need to with anyone else. I'm just getting the information I need, and we'll keep the Quip parked up here, but if I'm not back in . . . let's say a day, go and tell Artemis what's happened. There, do you feel better now?"

"A whole day?" Milo swallowed nervously.

"You've got enough to eat, I assume?" Horatio said.

"Yes, but—"

"Then you don't need to worry. The likelihood is that I'll be in and out before you've noticed that I've gone. The office and my sleeping quarters will of course be locked, but there's plenty of chores to be getting on with; I expect us to be ready to go as soon as I get back, and the cataloging of the Arthur Conan Doyle letters we got from Edinburgh to be finished." He waved his hand to signify he was done, and Milo turned toward the door.

"Actually, Milo, there's one more thing," Horatio called, and Milo stopped and turned back to face his uncle, who had a strange look on his face, as though he wasn't quite sure what to do, which was rare. He put his hand under his shirt collar and pulled out a gold chain from which a wooden whistle dangled.

Horatio pulled it over his head, stood up from his chair, and came to kneel in front of Milo. Milo felt hugely uncomfortable seeing his uncle so vulnerable and tried to take a step backward, but Horatio shook his head.

"Give me your hand," he said, and Milo slowly did as he was asked. His uncle turned his hand over so it was palm upward and put the whistle on its chain into it, closing Milo's fingers round it. "I will be needing this back the second . . ." He paused for emphasis. "The *second* I return, but I want you to keep it while I am gone. Just in case anything happens to me, or I do not come back, then you must use it. And above all you must not show it or give it to anyone else, including Artemis. Do you understand?"

"But I don't . . ."

"*Do you understand?*"

Milo nodded and slipped the chain over his head. Horatio looked deep into Milo's eyes and then stood up and returned to his desk, back to his gruff, closed self. "That's all."

12

One Thing at a Time

As they were still stationary at the Archive, Milo hopped back down onto the platform and then up into the engine cab to retrieve the scrapbook. He could feel the wood of the whistle warm against his skin, and he wanted to get back to the relative privacy of his own space to study it—and the scrapbook—while Horatio was away doing his research in the Record. He grabbed the book from the floor of the cab and shoved it back under his jumper before running the length of the platform to his own room.

Milo's carriage was very small and rather shabby, but it was the only space that had ever been his own entirely, and he loved it. As soon as he was safely through the door, he bolted it behind him and pulled the book out, putting it on his desk and making sure that none of the loose papers were at risk of falling out.

His bed was set against one wall and was previously the top half of a bunk bed, but Milo had removed the bottom bunk and turned it into a small desk. He had a tiny kitchen corner ("So you don't have to bother me every time you need feeding," according to Horatio) with a hot plate, a kettle, and a bucket of water that served as a fridge when Milo had ice to keep it cold. And there was a bookcase—of course—which was overflowing. Milo had decorated the space with various bits and pieces he'd collected: postcards and posters and even a string of Christmas lights that nearly all worked. The floor was covered in a patchy rug and mismatched cushions. Hester, the train cat, was asleep on one of them. They weren't quite sure where Hester had clambered aboard on their travels, but she had lived on the Quip for two years now. Not that Horatio ever acknowledged or fed her, but Milo was happy to have her company.

Opening his window a crack and pulling in a hose that was linked to a water butt on the roof of the train, Milo filled the kettle and set it on the hot plate to boil. He fished around for a clean-ish mug and popped a tea bag inside before picking up the scrapbook rather reverently and settling himself into the squashiest, comfiest cushion. Hester sleepily nestled into his leg.

The scrapbook was a large folio size and made of supple dark-brown leather. The pages inside were messily bound but made from thick, high quality paper. Horatio had trained Milo to notice things like this; he kept the intricacies of book smuggling and the magic of the Quip opaque, but he taught Milo a lot about books and printing so that he could help catalog and take care of the books that they stored onboard.

Milo unwound the cord that was keeping the scrapbook closed, and immediately sheets of loose paper spilled out: letters on thin yellow paper, newspaper articles, torn notes, official-looking records, even a photo or two. Milo felt like shoving it all back inside, closing the book, and hiding it away under his floorboards. It felt too big, to go from knowing so little to having so much information fall into his lap all at once. He stroked Hester's ginger fur and tried to calm his breathing.

"One thing at a time," he said to himself. He tidied the loose pages together into one pile before turning to the book itself, quickly realizing it was not even close to the formally compiled Records in the Archive; it really was just a scrapbook, the items inside stuck in neatly, sometimes with handwritten labels or notes. The beginning pages were much neater and more organized, and Milo felt his heart still when he saw the picture on the first page—a slightly blurry photo of a tiny baby in the arms of a happy but exhausted woman, with a besotted-looking man standing to her side.

It was him as a baby with his parents. "Milo Avi Bolt" was written underneath the photo, with his birthday.

There were more photos on the next few pages of Milo as a baby and his parents, and then . . . and then one of him in Horatio's arms, a younger, happier looking Horatio, although still with that wolfish glint in his eye. And then one of him being held by an older woman with white hair, a woman who stared at him with a face full of love and wonder.

"Who's that?" Milo whispered to himself, his finger tracing her face. There was no caption under the photo.

Apart from pictures, what there was most of were train tickets, all in different colors and languages, with routes from Paris to Venice, and somewhere called Flåm to Myrdal—both places Milo had never heard of. There were some photos of these trips too, mainly featuring his parents holding him up in front of train windows, grinning widely. Milo felt a tear escape and wiped it away roughly. Why on earth was this in the Archive, he thought to himself, and where did that mean his official white Record was—if he even had one at all?

After the more carefully assembled pages of photos and memorabilia, there were just blank pages, with a few loose items wedged into the binding. It wasn't hard to understand that the scrapbook had stopped being so carefully put together after his parents had died. He started looking through the rest of the information. There was a series of paper-clipped A4 reports from the Marters, with updates on how Milo was doing and requests for further payments. There were a few medical-looking forms and some crayon drawings.

And among this ephemera of a small life, there were things that were harder to understand: lists of names, lists of places, a map of a country with places Milo didn't recognize. There was a poster advertising "Evalina's Literary Curiosities," which featured a hand-drawn image of what looked an awful lot like the Quip and a photo that was *definitely* the Quip, although painted much more colorfully than it was now. There was also a thick piece of paper folded in three, with a broken wax seal and a small rectangular card with a strange symbol drawn on it—a circle with a bent and curved line inside it, like the wings of a bird in flight.

Milo had planned to try and sort the papers loosely into categories; there were things that were obviously to do with him as a child, things to do with the Quip, and things that he couldn't make head nor tail of. But as he was spreading the papers out on the floor of his carriage, a shout came.

"Milo? Where are you?"

Horatio was back already, and Milo had barely had a chance to read anything, or even look at the whistle on the chain. But there was nothing to be done, and right now he needed to clear the book up and hide it as quickly as possible. Milo hurriedly gathered the papers and shoved them messily back into the scrapbook, wincing as corners were bent and edges were ripped. He didn't have time to get the floorboard up and put the book in his secret hiding place, so he pushed it under the duvet on his bed, picked up a disgruntled Hester, and put her on top for good measure. Then, before Horatio could come and find him and see anything strange, he clambered up onto the top of the train and raced along the carriages, jumping easily over the gaps until he got to the office. He yanked open the door and arrived, breathless.

"I thought I told you to get sorting the Edinburgh papers?" Horatio said.

"You've only been gone for about fifteen minutes," Milo protested. "You said you'd be a day!"

"I said that if I was gone for a day then you should tell Artemis what had happened," Horatio said. "Will you ever learn to listen to the details? Now, my whistle?"

Milo pulled the chain from under his jumper, feeling an unexpected ache as the whistle stopped touching him, and passed it to his uncle, who put it back round his neck without any further comments.

"Did you find what you needed?" Milo asked.

"I did," Horatio said. "It confirmed my theory. And, as suspected, we are going to need Matilda Pages, in more ways than one. Fire up the Quip, Milo. We're heading to London."

13

A Business Arrangement

I t was hard for Milo to quench the uneasy feeling in his stomach as he hopped back into the engine cab and rolled two charged wooden orbs into the engine. He was excited to see Tilly but felt guilty for that, given the circumstances. Horatio's favors tended to be either dangerous, illegal, unethical, or all three at the same time. On top of all of that was the fact that he felt deeply unsettled because of the scrapbook and where he had found it and unnerved at the brief flash of camaraderie and trust when Horatio had given him the whistle to look after, even if it was just for a moment. That flash had almost been enough to tempt Milo into asking his uncle about the scrapbook, but he needed more time to look at what was inside before he would even know what questions he wanted to ask.

And now there was the issue of trying to keep Tilly as safe as possible.

It did not take too long for the Quip to reach London, and Horatio shouted for Milo to slow the train within the hour. Milo poked his head out of the window to see the shapes of north London starting to form in sparkling silhouettes as the Quip edged toward the boundary between Story and the outside world. It was like looking at the city through a thick fog.

"Where are we leaving the Quip?" asked Milo.

"We're heading straight to the bookshop."

"But won't there be people there?"

"If my calculations are right, and they usually are, it's just before nine o'clock in the evening in London, so they should be closed."

"Where are you putting the Quip, though? If we're both getting off, we'll need to stop properly."

"Enough questions," Horatio said sharply. "You should know by now that bookshops and libraries are much more flexible when it comes to space and boundaries. It comes from all the books, obviously. They're used to containing universes."

"Do you mean that for real?" Milo asked. "Or, like, as a metaphor?"

"Both," Horatio said. "How else do you think magic works?"

Every once in a while, Milo caught a glimpse in his uncle of some sort of enjoyment at what he did, or even playfulness. But it never lasted long, and if you tried to look directly at it, it immediately vanished and was unlikely to resurface for a good while.

True to his word, Horatio pulled the train up within the walls of Pages & Co. itself. And just as he said, there was no one there, and somehow the Quip just fitted. If you were listening carefully, you could hear the bookshelves sigh and creak a little as they made space and then settled again. Horatio climbed down onto the wooden floor of Pages & Co., and once Milo had jumped down after him he locked the office carriage carefully and pocketed the key.

"Shall we?" he said to Milo.

The majority of the bookshop lights were off, but the summer sun had not quite set, and the last of the late evening twilight illuminated the shining sides of the Quip among the shadows of the bookshop. There was a door outlined with light against one wall and the smell of something delicious in the air. The two of them approached the door in silence until they could hear a quiet, companionable murmur of conversation behind it. Horatio knocked firmly, and the chatter stopped abruptly. The door cracked open, and Elsie Pages peered out. She looked Horatio up and down suspiciously.

"Hello?" she said.

"Good evening," Horatio said smoothly. "You are Matilda's grandmother, I presume?"

"The more pressing question is who *you* are," Elsie said. "And what you are doing in my bookshop after our front door has been locked."

"We have alternative means of transport," Horatio said.

"Now, I must speak with you and your granddaughter."

"You won't be speaking to Tilly at all until you tell me more about—"

But she was interrupted by Tilly herself pushing the door further open. Her face blanched when she saw Horatio.

"Hello, Matilda," Horatio said, and Milo waved awkwardly.

"What . . . are you doing here?" Tilly said.

"I have come to discuss a business arrangement," Horatio said. "I am sure you have not forgotten that you promised me a

favor, which I am in need of calling in. I also believe that there is a matter I can assist you with—the health of your grandfather . . ."

Milo tried to keep the confusion off his face. What on earth did Tilly's grandfather have to do with any of this? What did he need help with?

"How do you know about Archie?" Elsie said, but she had relaxed her hold on the door. "What's your name? Who are you?"

"My name is Horatio Bolt," he answered with the very smallest dip of his head. "And I am the driver of the Sesquipedalian."

"Grandma, this is the man we told you about," Tilly said. "The man from the train—who helped us work out how to free the Source Editions." She sounded uncertain though, and Milo knew she was worrying about the favor—as she probably should be.

"Well, you may come in," Elsie said begrudgingly, and opened the door further.

Inside the warm kitchen was a large wooden table still strewn with the remnants of dinner. Milo smiled at Tilly, who raised a wary eyebrow at him. Milo shrugged in response, wishing he could talk to her in private before his uncle no doubt ruined everything. Horatio hadn't mentioned anything about Tilly's grandfather to him, and Milo couldn't help but notice that Archie wasn't present in the kitchen. There were only two other people in the room: Tilly's mother, Bea, who Milo had met, and a woman with brown skin and long black hair who he didn't recognize. His uncle, however, was thrown by the sight of the second woman, just for a fraction of a second.

"Might I have the honor of meeting Ms. Amelia Whisper, Librarian of the British Underlibrary?" he said, and only Milo could detect the hint of sarcasm in his voice. His uncle did not have much time for the rules and regulations of the Underlibraries or the people who ran them.

Amelia Whisper gave a nod of her head. "And you have me at a disadvantage, as I do not know you," she said.

"My name is Horatio Bolt," Milo's uncle said again.

"Ah," Amelia said. "In which case, I do know who you are. Tilly and Bea have filled me in."

"I assure you I'm here to help," Horatio replied.

"I think that remains to be seen," said Elsie.

14

The Ideal Circumstances for a Partnership

"Now, before we begin," Elsie said, "would you like a cup of tea? And have you eaten?" she asked gently, turning to Milo.

"We're fine," Horatio said, answering for both of them, but Elsie looked carefully at Milo, and a few moments later she slid a plate of hot buttered toast and a glass of milk in front of him, shaking her head as he tried to say no or thank you—he wasn't sure which.

Horatio let it pass. "Now, I'm not sure what Matilda has told you about the events that took place a few months ago," he said, sitting down without being asked.

"That you helped work out the Underwoods' weakness and that your knowledge of *book magic* helped Tilly to free the bound Source editions," Elsie said carefully.

"We also know that you

operate outside the knowledge or approval of the Underlibraries," Amelia said, raising an eyebrow. Milo noticed that she had the suggestion of a smile on her lips, but his uncle wouldn't respond well to anything that sounded even remotely like a threat or a judgment.

Thankfully, Bea jumped in before Horatio could rise to Amelia's bait. "I know that you claim you acted only in your own self-interest," she said. "And that your goals just happened to overlap with ours, but I think you knew it was the right thing to do." She smiled, trying to make him feel welcome.

"I am aware you intend that as a compliment," Horatio said, a little awkwardly. "But I assure you none of this has to do with right and wrong."

"He did bring the Underwoods boxes of Source Editions for them to destroy," Tilly pointed out to her mother. "And those books would have gone forever . . . and some of them did." She turned to Horatio. "And you made me promise you a favor or you wouldn't bring us home. So . . ."

"Now about this favor," Elsie said, a protective hand on Tilly's shoulder. "Let's hear what you have come here to say, Mr. Bolt, but let's not have any pretense that an agreement made with a twelve-year-old child while they were reliant on you to get them home safely is in *any* way legally or morally binding." She fixed Horatio with a piercing stare that he could not hold.

"Well," he went on, "let me set out what I have come to talk to you about and progress from there. I believe we can come to a mutually helpful arrangement. Indeed, there are several ways we can currently help each other, the ideal circumstances for a partnership. I believe that you are in possession of a book I am interested in, and yes, I also have need of Matilda's ability to remove things from books, and, finally, I also believe I have access to the information that will allow you to cure your husband, father, and grandfather, Archibald."

Milo dropped his piece of toast onto his plate. "Your grandad is poorly?" he asked, worried.

"Yes, he—" Tilly started, but her grandmother cut in.

"How did you hear about Archie?" Elsie asked Horatio quietly. "Only a very few trusted friends are aware of his condition."

"You have not taken him to see a doctor, I take it?" Horatio asked.

"No," Amelia said. "We have enough understanding of magic to realize this is not a simple medical problem. He's been unconscious without food or drink for two weeks, but he is still breathing—he's clearly in some sort of magical suspension or something. I don't think the local GP would be able to help, somehow."

"May I see him?" Horatio asked.

Elsie and Amelia exchanged a look, and Amelia gave a shrug.

"If it will help you help him then I don't see the harm," Elsie said slowly as if looking for the trap in Horatio's request. "Come on. He's upstairs."

Elsie opened the door that led to the stairs and gestured for Horatio to follow her. Tilly glanced at Milo and then beckoned that he should come too. Curious about Archie's state and eager for the chance to speak to Tilly, Milo pushed his chair back and followed them up a flight of stairs to a door, which Elsie pushed open quietly.

The room was not large when all of them were standing in it. A fresh vase of flowers stood on a side table, and the window was cracked open to let in the evening air. On the bed was Archie Pages, looking as though he were simply having a nap. Milo could see his chest rising and falling, and his eyes were flickering under his eyelids. His skin was pale apart from his fingertips, which were stained a dark purple, looking unnatural and strange in the cozy bedroom setting.

Horatio stepped closer to Archie and peered at his stained fingers, Elsie eyeing him closely all the while. Meanwhile, Tilly tugged on Milo's jumper sleeve and pulled him back out into the corridor.

"Hi," she said. She sounded tired and worried, and Milo wished that he wasn't always appearing at the most stressful and scary points of her bookwandering adventures. "You really didn't know?" she asked quietly.

"No, I promise," Milo said. "I didn't even know we were

coming here until this morning. You know he doesn't tell me anything."

"Is Grandad going to be okay?" Tilly asked.

"I don't know," Milo said. "I really don't."

"I just hoped you might have some sort of idea, or you might have seen something similar." Tilly shrugged.

"I'm sorry," Milo said, feeling utterly useless. "But Horatio really does know quite a bit about magical poisons and stuff. He finds loads of books about them for one of his clients who's a botanist—I wouldn't be surprised if it was her who had the cure."

"Really?" Tilly looked more hopeful.

"Really," Milo said. "I mean, I don't know for sure, and I also know that Horatio is hard to trust, but if he wants something, then that's when you should believe him—even if he's not letting on the whole story."

"So we should agree to whatever deal he's going to suggest?" Tilly asked him.

"I . . . I . . ." Milo didn't know what to say. Tilly was putting too much responsibility and trust in him, and he had no idea what his uncle was planning. "Maybe?" he ended up saying, disappointed in himself.

"I guess we'll just see what he says," Tilly said. "I just want Grandad to be okay. Amelia is doing all this research, taking samples and doing tests, and reading all these old books, but I don't think she's found much that's useful so far. Not that they tell me as much as I want to know, as per usual. If they'd just trust me with a bit more information or give me more to do—I just feel so helpless. The thing is—"

But she was stopped from telling Milo the thing as Horatio and Elsie emerged from the bedroom, and the four of them headed back downstairs to the kitchen.

"Clearly, he has been poisoned," Horatio said, once they were all sitting round the kitchen table again. "You are right—he is being held in some kind of imagined suspension. It's an intricate and clever thing to try, and the person I suspect is behind it is a very dangerous and ambitious man."

Elsie and Amelia's faces dropped. Bea looked close to tears.

"But I have good news," said Horatio. "I can cure him."

15

An Unspecified, Probably Dangerous, Journey

There was silence for a moment as they stared at Horatio.

"That is quite a promise," Elsie said. "And, of course, you know it's something we're desperate for. I won't pretend otherwise. But I want to know what you want from us before we proceed."

"From you, I need Matilda, and I would also like the book that poisoned Archie," Horatio explained. "I am assuming it was a copy of *The Wizard of Oz*?"

Amelia blinked. "How could you kn—?" she began.

"It is my job to trade in knowledge," Horatio said. "Surely my understanding of the situation ought to convince you of my ability to help?"

"Why do you want the book?" Elsie asked.

"Several reasons," Horatio said. "But one of them is that I need to be able to analyze the poison, if I am to cure Archibald.

I told you it was an intricate thing; it is not so simple as giving you some sort of antidote I have prepared and ready."

"I can see the logic in that," Elsie admitted. "Although you seem very confident you can cure him given that you don't yet know exactly how the poison works. I think there is something you're not telling us. And the book is our only clue as to what has happened. If you take it away, we have no recourse to do any research of our own."

"You will *have* to trust me," Horatio said, and Elsie did not try to disguise her snort of disbelief. "But I would have thought that if you trusted me with Matilda, you would let me take the book and bring you the cure."

"You are presuming we trust you with anything," Elsie said.

"Not to mention that it's obviously absolutely out of the question for Tilly to go anywhere with you," Bea added firmly.

"What we mean is that we will of course need a chance to discuss this privately," Elsie said, giving her daughter a look. "It goes without saying that if this is even to be taken seriously as an arrangement, we will be accompanying Matilda at all points."

"That is not the deal I am offering," Horatio said. "Matilda will come on her own."

"You expect us to let you take her alone, on an unspecified, probably dangerous, journey, to steal something for you? It's absolutely beyond reason," Elsie said.

"Don't I get a say?!" Tilly said. "I want to help Grandad. I've been on the Quip before, and it was fine. Ish."

"You see, Matilda understands that this is a business trans-
action," Horatio said. "That I must get something in return
for helping you. You will let Matilda come with me because I
will then be able to wake Archibald. As I said, it's an excellent
arrangement because we both need each other, and therefore
there is no reason for either of us to default."

"Except that there's nothing stopping you from changing
your mind once Tilly has helped you," Amelia pointed out. "And
then you might—"

"I'll do it," Tilly cut in. "What if this is the only chance we
get to help Grandad?" she pleaded, turning to her mother and
grandmother.

"I don't believe that it will be," Elsie said quietly. "We have
Amelia working on it at the Underlibrary. It may take a little
longer, but Archie seems to be safe as he is."

Milo watched her as she closed her eyes and breathed in
deeply. He had no doubt that Horatio would trade an errand
from him for something he wanted without a second thought,
and yet Elsie would keep Tilly safe even if it meant that her
husband would stay poisoned.

"How about a different arrangement?" Bea offered, exchang-
ing a quick look with her mother. "We give you the book, and
you help us with the cure. A direct trade. The book for the cure."

"No. I need Matilda's skills," Horatio said firmly.

"Okay, okay," Elsie said, setting her hands flat on the table
and fixing Horatio with that determined gaze. "We will give you

the book. And if you can provide us with some sort of evidence that you are able to help cure Archie, then we can rediscuss the arrangement. Although I assure you it will never involve Tilly going anywhere without one of us. But, with some proof that you can help, we can perhaps keep negotiating and work something out. We will give you the copy of *The Wizard of Oz* as a gesture of our good faith, and we will wait for you to produce a reciprocal gesture of your own. Do you accept?"

"I cannot promise that the cure will be as effective with this delay," Horatio said. "Are you willing to accept that risk?"

"Grandma, no," Tilly said, looking horribly guilty, but Elsie kept her eyes on Horatio. She swallowed and nodded.

"I am," she said.

16

More Than One Story

ilo looked at his uncle, who was maintaining Elsie's stare. He knew his uncle was wanting to make some clever remark back, but he also knew that Horatio was willing to constantly reassess and reanalyze deals and relationships to get what he wanted.

"I agree," Horatio said sharply, standing up and holding out his hand. "If I am able to take the book with me now, I will return with proof that I can help Archibald, and then we will negotiate the terms of Matilda helping me. Let us leave it at that for now. The book?"

Elsie nodded, shook his hand, and disappeared upstairs again.

The five of them sat in awkward silence while she was gone. Milo was desperate to continue talking to Tilly but couldn't think of anything he could say in front of the adults, and so had to settle for giving her a small smile, which he was relieved to see her return. Bea simply sat and glared icily at Horatio.

Elsie returned downstairs a few moments later holding a clear plastic bag with an old clothbound book inside. Without a word, she passed it to Horatio, who nodded his thanks and gestured at Milo to follow him out of the cozy kitchen. As they were leaving, Milo looked over his shoulder to try and wave good-bye to Tilly, but she was sitting staring into space with a distracted, sad look on her face, and Horatio had closed the door behind them before she looked back his way.

Horatio stalked back to the Quip in long, angry strides.

"Well, at least you got the book you wanted," Milo tried, running after him.

"You have no idea what we're dealing with," Horatio snapped, as he yanked the key from his pocket and wrenched the door of his office open. He climbed up the steps and threw the book in the bag onto his desk. "There is so much more at stake than you know, and I *need* Matilda. He's not going to be happy with . . ." He stopped and took a deep breath. "But, as you say, we have this, and this is something."

"Is the poison thingy you need inside there?" Milo asked.

"Yes," Horatio said, running his hand through his hair with worry. "Sort of. It's in every copy, in his hidden library— you can get in through any Emerald City—he controls them all." He looked Milo up and down. "There is more than one story happening here, Milo. It's important you understand that.

The Botanist and I have been working on . . . something that is vital, but it has to be kept secret. We need to understand how the poison works, otherwise we'll never stop him."

"Stop who?" Milo asked in confusion.

Horatio waved this away. "The Botanist needs to know more, and she needs the poison compendium. Milo, do you understand?"

"No! I don't understand at all!" Milo said hopelessly. "You never tell me anything."

"I'm trying to keep you safe," Horatio said shortly. "That's all you need to know."

"But from what?"

"From *who*," Horatio said, sounding a little manic. "You need to trust me. I have a plan. The Botanist and I have a plan. But I need Matilda for it to work. And we need to get further before he works out what we're doing. There are too many threads—I can't keep hold of them all before time runs out and everything is out in the open."

"Maybe I could help?" Milo said.

"You were supposed to help convince Matilda to come with us," Horatio said. "The compendium is vital, only Matilda can get it out of *The Wizard of Oz*. The Botanist needs what's inside."

Milo could barely follow what his uncle was saying as Horatio paced and paced, speaking more to himself than Milo now. It was rare and unsettling to see Horatio in such a state of distress when he was usually so composed, regardless of what was happening around him. As his uncle paced and muttered and cursed, talking through whatever complicated plan he had concocted with the Botanist, he seemed to forget that Milo was even there.

It was clear that the poison compendium was important though, and that it was inside *The Wizard of Oz*, and crucially, most bookwanderers wouldn't be able to get it out.

"But how does this man you're talking about even get stuff out of this hidden library?" Milo asked. His uncle was so focused on Tilly because her ability was so rare, maybe even unique. What use was it if anything taken inside was stuck there?

"He might use Bookmarks, like we do sometimes," Horatio said. "You know that people can take out the thing they took into a book, so if I send someone in to hide something, they stay there and guard it and can bring it out when I need it. But, honestly, I would be very surprised if he hadn't worked out some concoction that allows him to take things out of books himself. He has found a way to break so many rules already. Now let me think, boy. I need to work out what to do."

Milo edged over to the desk and stared at the book, wondering where the library was hidden and how it was kept secret in such a famous story. He picked up the clear bag and pulled it open, peering in, trying to see if he could see anything unusual. The plastic crinkled noisily, and Horatio whipped his head round.

"You fool!" Horatio yelled, barreling into him, seizing the bag and knocking him over onto the floor.

Milo tried not to cry as he stared up at his uncle, who was

now touching the poisoned book, which had fallen half out of the bag. Horatio looked back at Milo in horror, dropping the book onto the floor, but it was too late.

"What were you doing?" Horatio whispered.

"I'm so sorry," Milo cried in horror. "I wasn't going to touch it—I was just looking!"

"Never listening," Horatio said hoarsely, starting to sweat profusely and leaning hard against his desk. "Listen . . . carefully . . . now. The whistle . . . Take the Quip. You must not trust . . ." He descended into a huge coughing fit and dropped heavily to his knees.

"Who mustn't I trust?" Milo begged, crawling toward his uncle, who waved him aggressively away.

"Don't touch . . . Poison . . ." Horatio gasped. "Get the poison . . . compendium. Matilda can . . . remove it. Take it to . . . Botanist."

"The Botanist can help?" Milo asked wretchedly, tears running down his cheeks.

Horatio just managed to nod. "You can trust her."

"But who is the poisoner?" Milo said desperately. "Who can't I trust?"

But Horatio couldn't get any more words out before he went
        very,
            very pale
                and collapsed.

TILLY

17

One More Letter

These sorts of situations called for a best friend, and so Tilly went up to her bedroom and phoned hers.

"Heyyyy," Oskar sing-songed as he picked up. "It's late—are you okay?"

"Kind of," she said. "I mean, I'm totally safe, but you'll never guess who turned up at Pages & Co. after dinner."

"Ooooh, okay, was it the Mad Hatter?" Oskar guessed. "Or the Very Hungry Caterpillar? Or Paddington? I hope it was Paddington."

"No, no, no," Tilly said, laughing despite her worries about her grandad. "It wasn't a character from a book—it was Horatio and Milo Bolt—from the Quip."

"They were at Pages?" Oskar said in surprise. "Why didn't you tell me! I would have come over!"

"I doubt your mum would have let you at this time, and they were only here for about twenty minutes, if that," Tilly said.

"What did they want?"

"It was strange. Horatio knew that my grandad was poorly. He said he knew he'd been poisoned and that he could help."

"Well, that's good—isn't it?"

"Yeah, but you know what he's like, he wanted two things in return. He wanted the book that poisoned Grandad in the first place, and he wanted me to go with him to help him get something *out* of a book. He said he was calling in the favor."

"I'm sure that went down *suuuper* well with Bea and Elsie," Oskar said.

"Exactly, they obviously wouldn't let me go. But they gave him the book, and they said that if he could come back and prove that he could cure Grandad then we could talk more and maybe I could go if one of them came with me."

"Well, that sounds like a good plan then," Oskar said. "I'm gutted I missed it. If you do go with him, you have to let me come too."

"Except that Horatio *also* said that the delay might mean the cure wouldn't work," she said.

"Ah," Oskar said.

"So, what if it's all my fault that we don't get help in time?" Tilly said. "What if I could have done something to help him?"

"None of this is your fault," Oskar said quickly. "Whoever

sent that stupid book in the first place—that's whose fault it is. And you know what Horatio's like; he'll say whatever he needs to get what he wants."

"I know, but it's impossible to just ignore what he said about time."

"I get it, but you don't have any choice now he's gone anyway," Oskar pointed out. "Unless you . . . No, that's not a good idea."

"What's not a good idea?"

"Well, you said Milo was there, that he heard the whole conversation?"

"Yep," Tilly agreed. "We didn't get to speak by ourselves for long, but he said that if his uncle's getting something he wants, he's probably telling the truth about being able to help."

"Well, why don't you write to him? Ask him if he thinks you should go."

"I would, but there's no point! We've tried writing to him like he told us to—how many notes have we addressed to him and put in the back of a book? Maybe he was just making a joke about it being able to get to him via the Endpapers."

"But the notes all disappear!" Oskar said. "They're going somewhere!"

"Well, either it's not working, or he doesn't care," Tilly said. "I wish I'd thought to ask him about it earlier."

"It's got to be worth trying one more time for something like this," Oskar pointed out. "For your grandad."

"Okay . . . but what if he *does* think I should go?"

"Then maybe you should go?" Oskar said. "We both know that you want to. Tell Milo that if *he* thinks it's a good idea, he can tell his uncle you're in, and that you'll sneak out and wait in the shop for them to pick you up."

"That's a good plan," said Tilly. "It will have to be later though, otherwise Mum and Grandma will know. I'll say I'll be in the shop at midnight."

"Great," Oskar said. "I'm just so gutted I can't come too."

"Okay. One more letter," Tilly agreed. "For Grandad."

"So, the only other thing I need to know is, if you do go with them, and Elsie calls me and asks if I know where you've gone, which she obviously will," Oskar said, "how long do you want me to leave it before I tell them the truth?"

"Well, time works differently in Story." Tilly thought it through out loud. "And I don't know what the plan is yet, or what Horatio wants me to do. But if it's just going into a book and getting something out, I reckon I could be there and back again before breakfast."

"Quite possibly," said Oskar. "We were barely gone at all when we went to find the Archivists. But, just in case, I'll give it a day. And, remember, when you get back, none of this was my idea."

"Thanks, Oskar," Tilly said, and they hung up.

Tilly grabbed a notebook and pen from her desk and began to write.

Dear Milo,

It was really nice to see you earlier. I'm sorry that we didn't get a chance to talk more. I don't know if you've been getting our letters. If we're just annoying you, I guess you can ignore this one too, but I'm writing about the whole deal your uncle was trying to make about the thing he needs to get out of a book.

You said you thought he would be telling the truth if he needed something out of it, so I wanted to ask if you thought I should do it. My grandad is really poorly, and if there's a way to help him, I have to try, even if my grandma and mum don't know. I'm not sure how you can get a letter back to me or if you will even see this, so, if you really do think that it's not a trick or a trap, maybe you could tell your uncle to come back to Pages & Co. and pick me up? I think I'd be okay if you were there too.

But we need to wait until Grandma and Mum have gone to bed, so I'll wait in the bookshop for an hour from midnight tonight, and if you don't come, I'll assume you haven't told your uncle and we'll stick to the original plan.

I hope we get a chance to see you soon, whatever happens. Oskar says hi!

Tilly

Feeling a little silly, she folded the paper and picked up the nearest book. Opening it to the endpapers, the bit between the very last page and the cover, Tilly slid the note in. Closing the book tight, she waited for her letter to disappear, as it had every time that she and Oskar had tried it, without ever getting a message back. Maybe Milo just didn't have access to whatever post box this turned up in, and this whole Endpapers message system couldn't work.

Oh well, she thought to herself. *We'll see.*

While she was waiting for midnight, Tilly packed a book, some cereal bars, and her phone charger—although she had no idea if there was any electricity onboard the Quip. She wondered how electricity and imagination worked together. Hearing her grandma's voice in her mind, she also grabbed her toothbrush and a spare pair of socks. Nothing wrong with being prepared—even though she knew deep down that she wasn't really expecting them to see her note and come back for her.

She got changed into jeans and a warm striped jumper and got her boots ready to go, before jumping into bed and pretending to be asleep when her mum came to check on her. She didn't want to risk a nap or her phone alarm waking anyone else up, so once she had heard the rest of the house go through the bathroom and to their own bedrooms, she read a few chapters of her book with her flashlight under the duvet.

When it was nearly midnight, she put the flashlight into her

bag, picked up her boots, and tiptoed downstairs in her socks. Thankfully, the door to the shop opened quietly, and she closed it carefully behind her before turning into the dark bookshop. She had to clap her free hand over her mouth to stifle a shout because there already, curled up in the dark like a *sleeping* dragon, was the Quip.

Despite the inarguable presence of the train itself, there was no sign of Horatio and Milo, so Tilly crept up to the carriage at the front of the train. She gave the door a gentle knock, but no one answered. She tried again, a little louder, and the door was flung open to reveal a wild-eyed Milo, his curly hair messy and his face flushed.

"What do you want?" he said in a panicked hiss.

"Didn't you get my note?" Tilly said in confusion.

"What note?!" Milo said, sticking his head out of the train and looking around. "I didn't get a note!"

"But . . . I sent it via the Endpapers, like you said!" Tilly protested. "Why are you here if you didn't get it?"

"We never left!" Milo said, his voice considerably more high-pitched than usual. "Never mind that! Quick, come on!" He reached out for Tilly's hand but got her boots instead, which she was still holding. He glanced at them in confusion before throwing them behind him and reached again to grab her wrist. Tilly clambered awkwardly up, and Milo slammed the door shut behind her.

"What on earth is going on?" Tilly said, looking at him in distress. "Are you okay? Shall I get my mum?"

"No!" Milo hissed. "And turn round!"

Tilly spun and immediately could see what was wrong. On the floor in an undignified heap was Horatio Bolt. He was unconscious but breathing, and the tips of his fingers were stained **deep purple.**

18

A Good, Inspiring Speech

"Oh no," Tilly whispered.

"IS HE DEAD?" Milo said, breathing very hard and quickly.

"No!" Tilly said. "If he's been poisoned with the book, then surely he'll be in the same state as Grandad, in a sleep we can't wake him from. But why on earth did he touch the book? He knows it's poisoned. I don't understand."

"It's my fault," Milo said forlornly. "I was just looking at it, but Horatio thought I was going to take it out of the bag and shoved me out of the way, and it fell out. He got poisoned to stop me touching it."

Tilly watched as the realization dawned on Milo's face. "He saved me. I wouldn't have thought he would do that, you know?"

"I think you should sit down," Tilly said gently. "And I know he isn't always very . . . kind, but clearly he loves you deep down or he wouldn't have risked himself to stop you getting poisoned. No offense, but he really doesn't seem like the type to do that for someone he doesn't care about."

"None of it makes sense," Milo said, letting Tilly lead him round to his uncle's chair. "Hang on . . . You said you wrote to me?"

"Yes!" Tilly said. "Oskar and I have written to you loads of times! But obviously we were doing it wrong somehow. This evening I wrote to you to say that if it wasn't a trick or a trap, could you tell your uncle to come pick me up so I could do what he wanted and get the cure for my grandad. But I guess we need it for *both* of them now, so I hope he's explained a bit more to you. And we need to get the train *out* of the shop before Mum comes down to open it!"

"But I don't know how to drive it!" Milo wailed. "I don't know anything at all!"

"I'm sure that's not true," Tilly said, trying to stay calm for her own benefit as much as Milo's. Maybe she should just go and wake up her mum or grandma. If she could get into her pajamas on the way, she could say she'd been sleepwalking or something, and no one would need to know anything about her letter or her half-thought-through plan, and Grandma would be able to look after Milo.

But she just kept hearing Horatio's words echoing in her head about time, and much as she loved her grandma, past experience had taught her that however much was on the line, her grandma would always try to do things the proper and sensible way, and there just wasn't time for that.

"First things first. You need to get us out of here," she said to Milo as confidently as she could. "You must have picked up *something* about how the train works. Is there anything at all that Horatio told you or gave you, or is there an instruction manual somewhere or something?"

"An instruction manual for a secret, magical train?" Milo said in amazement.

"You never know!" Tilly said. "I think everything should come with instructions."

"Hang on," Milo said slowly, grabbing Tilly's wrist. "The whistle."

"Ow!" she said, yanking it back. "What whistle?"

But Milo didn't reply, only stood up shakily and knelt beside his uncle's crumpled body. He didn't move for a moment, then took a deep breath and looked back at Tilly.

"Before we do anything else, please could you help me put him somewhere safe and comfortable?"

"Of course," Tilly said at once, and rushed to Milo's side. "Where do you want to put him?"

"In his carriage," Milo said. "We'll need . . ." He tailed off and reached forward, pulling a large ring of keys out of Horatio's coat pocket. "These. Okay, so maybe if you take his legs and I pick him up under his shoulders, we can carry him? It's only the next carriage. I'll go and unlock it first." He stood up and darted away with the keys, leaving Tilly with the unconscious Horatio. Milo's uncle was definitely breathing, although it was very slow. Tilly couldn't help but notice that he looked much kinder when he was asleep.

Well, she thought to herself, *either Milo will work out how to drive this thing and we'll find the cure by ourselves, or he won't, in which case the only answer is to tell Grandma and Mum. Either way, that's a plan.* And, as usual, she felt a bit better once there was a plan.

Milo returned quickly and gave her a nod. Tilly tried not to think too much about it and took a firm hold of Horatio's ankles as Milo tried to get a good grip under his uncle's armpits. It was not a dignified way to travel, and from what Tilly knew of Horatio, she imagined he would hate it. He was a tall man and heavy for two children to carry, but between them they half carried, half dragged him down the length of the office.

It was only a small gap between this carriage and the next, but it was the most precarious bit of the trip, not helped by the narrow doorways. Tilly let Horatio's legs dangle in the gap and jumped across before kneeling down and grabbing them again. The thought crossed her mind that if the situation wasn't so scary, it almost might have been funny, like something out of the old Laurel and Hardy films that Grandad loved. That thought was quickly erased when she banged her elbow hard and painfully on the side of Horatio's bed, but soon she and

Milo had managed to get him on top of it. Milo straightened out his limbs so he really did look like he was only sleeping. He also very carefully reached into Horatio's shirt and pulled out a wooden whistle on a chain. Milo gently raised his uncle's head and slipped the chain over it, putting the whistle round his own before marching quickly back into the office.

"So, you mentioned the whistle might be important?" Tilly said tentatively, after Milo had been standing, shell-shocked, in the middle of the carriage for nearly a minute.

"What?" he said, looking at her as if she'd just arrived. "Sorry, yes, I did." He pulled the chain from under his jumper and showed her. "When Horatio bookwandered into the Record—I'll tell you about that bit in a moment," he said, seeing Tilly about to interrupt with a question. "So, anyway, when he did, just before he went, he gave me this whistle to look after. He's never done that before, and he told me that if anything happened to him, I should keep it secret and keep it safe."

"So, what does it do?" Tilly said. "Sorry, can I ask questions now?"

"Sure, but I won't know any of the answers," Milo said.

"You'll definitely know more than me," Tilly said, suddenly very aware of how little she knew about regular trains, let alone magical ones. "I don't even know what train whistles are for normally—aren't they just to let people know they're coming?"

"But there has to be a reason Horatio has it and keeps it on him *and* keeps it secret," Milo said. "It must be really important."

"You think it has to do with driving the train?" Tilly said.

"It must do," Milo said. "And it's made out of wood," he pointed out, "which is the best way to conduct *book magic*."

"Well, why don't you blow it and see?" Tilly said, not sure how else they would work out if it did nothing.

"I can't just blow it and see what happens!" Milo said, horrified.

"Why not?"

"Well, because . . ." He tailed off.

"Because you feel silly?" Tilly said, and Milo nodded. "When Oskar and I were looking for the Archive, there were all sorts of things that felt silly or that people around us told us were nonsense, but you have to follow what you feel in your heart. I know it sounds cheesy, but it really does work. If you think that this whistle means something, then go for it. And, you know, if nothing happens, then it's no big deal, and we'll go and wake up my family."

"Okay," Milo said, giving her a small smile. "That was a good speech, by the way."

"My grandad has always taught me the value of a good inspiring speech," she said, trying to smile, but the thought of her grandad, lying unconscious, just like Horatio, made her feel all wrong and cold inside, and Horatio's warning about time played again in her head.

"Okay, here goes," Milo said. He put the whistle to his lips and blew.

19

You Just Need to Imagine

 here was no sound, and Tilly tried to quell her disappointment, not wanting to put Milo off. He tried again, with a bit more confidence, but there was still no noise.

"It doesn't even work," Milo said, embarrassed. "Let's try . . ." But before he could finish Tilly felt something.

"Did the train just move?" she said, eyes alight.

"It felt like it . . . wriggled?" Milo said, and he was right: it felt like the stretch you do when you've just woken up from a really good nap.

"Do it again! Blow the whistle again!" Tilly said, and so Milo did. But this time, instead of a sort of satisfied sleepy stretch, the sensation was more of a shake, a reprimand.

"Sorry, sorry!" Milo said. "Okay, I'll stop with the whistle."

"I guess you've got her attention now," Tilly said. "If you

carry on, it's like keeping ringing someone's doorbell even after they've opened the door. You need to tell her where to go!" She was fizzing with excitement and hope.

"And how exactly do you suggest I do that?" Milo said. "Hang on . . ."

Tilly watched as he closed his eyes and his forehead creased into a frown. "What are you doing?" she whispered.

"I think I just . . . This sounds ridiculous, but given what fuels her I don't suppose it could be as easy as just . . . imagining it?"

"I don't see why not," Tilly said. "Maybe the whistle makes you the driver? Whoever uses it sets the destination? And that's why Horatio keeps it so well hidden? Imagine where you want to go! Quick, before she goes back to sleep or turns off or whatever you call it!"

Milo closed his eyes.

"Hang on," Tilly said. "Where *do* we want to go?"

But it was too late because all of a sudden there was a shaking deep in the bones of the Quip, and it lurched forward abruptly, sending Tilly and Milo tumbling to the floor.

"Did it work?" Milo said, trying to get his balance, but the train was still jolting forward in fits and starts, and it was hard to stay upright. "Did I do it?"

"You did something—that's for sure," Tilly said. She staggered over to one of the windows and pulled up the blinds. It was almost like they were traveling through a huge flip-book with different places flashing past them so quickly it was hard to tell where they were.

"This . . . doesn't feel like it does when Horatio is driving," said Milo a little shakily.

"Well, we're definitely going somewhere," Tilly said, holding tight to the window frame to stop herself from falling. "But you're right, this isn't what it looked like last time—what were you thinking about when it worked?"

"Um, I'm not sure," Milo said. "I was feeling quite over-whelmed by everything, and I couldn't focus. I was still trying to decide where to imagine when she started moving." He joined Tilly at the window and looked out in alarm. The train was juddering and jolting around them, and they watched helplessly as they flashed past a castle on a clifftop, through an old city, across an ocean, then a desert—all far too quickly to tell where anywhere was. It was almost as if the train couldn't think straight or work out how to get wherever Milo was imagining.

Tilly tried not to panic. "Well, okay, you've never driven the train before, so of course it's going to take a little bit of getting used to," she said, clinging on tightly. "The important thing is that you clearly can do it! So . . ." She paused, a horrible thought occurring to her. "Is this my fault?" she asked in a small voice.

"Why on earth would it be *your* fault?" Milo said in surprise.

"Well, you remember how I was having all those problems with stories coming out of their books and trying to take me back with them?"

"Oh yeah—is that still happening?"

"Nowhere near as often—we thought maybe when we freed so many of the Source Editions that had helped. But every once in a while, something spills out, and I still have to be on the lookout for plants and stuff trying to grab me."

"I don't think this is that, though," Milo said. "But I don't know! The whole point of the Quip is to allow us to safely travel through Story. It shouldn't be trying to get you in here!"

"But, if it's not me, then what's happening? Is it to do with the engine? Do you have to—I don't know—light it or something, or put more *book magic* in?"

"The engine!" Milo shouted. "Of course! Why can't I do anything right? I've no idea how much magic is even in the engine. I bet that's it."

The two of them tried to keep themselves steady as they climbed into the engine car. Milo opened the hatch to the engine, and they could see that although there were still smoldering embers, there was no fire roaring.

"There's nowhere near enough power for us to get anywhere," Milo said, relieved. "I'm not sure how we're moving so fast without any fuel, but this must be the problem, right?" Tilly shrugged in what she hoped was an encouraging way; she had no idea. The Quip seemed to gleefully refuse to follow any logic she could get to grips with.

Milo turned and picked up some of the charged wooden orbs and rolled them into the engine, where they almost immediately caught fire and started sparking. He glanced back at the net of orbs.

"We're going to need to charge some more soon," he said nervously.

"That's fine. We can do that—I've done it before!" Tilly said, starting to feel calmer. But as the orbs started to burn more fiercely and release their *book magic*, instead of the train easing into a steadier motion, she simply picked up pace, jolting them around even more dramatically.

"Milo, you have to try again," Tilly urged him. "You have to try and clearly imagine somewhere to go!"

"But I don't know where!"

"Can you just think of somewhere safe?" Tilly said.

"We just left somewhere safe!" Milo wailed. "We should never have gone and now we'll never get back!"

"That's not true!" Tilly said, trying to sound firmer and calmer than she felt.

"Maybe you should have a go," Milo was saying. "In fact, I don't know why you didn't do it to start with—the whole half-fictional thing might come in handy. You could probably talk directly to Story."

"Listen to me, Milo!" Tilly insisted. "I don't know this

train—you've spent half your life on her, and she knows *you*. I don't think just anyone can drive her. You just need to imagine!"

"Maybe I don't have a powerful enough imagination," Milo said hopelessly.

"The situation would seem to suggest that, if anything, it's *too* powerful," Tilly said as she hung desperately on to the net.

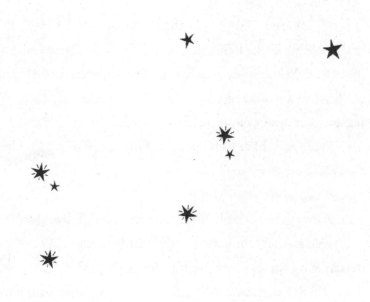

★ 20 ★

Hot CHocolate Always Helps

The pace of the Quip didn't let up, and it was burning through the *book magic* incredibly quickly. It continued jumping through place after place without letting up, and no amount of blowing on the whistle or imagining from either of them seemed to stop the train or slow it down.

"Shall we just let it burn through the *book magic* and see where it stops?" Tilly suggested, not quite sure what else there was to do at this point. Milo gave a despondent nod of agreement. "All these places we're traveling through . . ." Tilly said, her curiosity overtaking as they raced on. "Are they *inside* books too? A moment ago, I wondered if we went through the Mad Hatter's tea party, but I only caught a glimpse."

"Not quite," Milo said. "We can't go inside books on the train, much to Horatio's annoyance—we still have to book-wander in the traditional way. But we're traveling through imagination, so maybe we're seeing flashes of all the ideas and stories that make up Story. I don't think we could actually stop in any of them. The Endpapers seem to rebuff us."

"And the Endpapers are different from Story?" Tilly asked, not quite sure how it all fit together.

"Yup," Milo said. "It's all kind of made of the same stuff, as far as I know, but Story is, like, all of everything; it's all of space and time; it's existed from the very beginning because people have told each other stories since the very beginning. And then the Endpapers are to do with books themselves, the physical objects, which are obviously the most common way to hold stories but not the only one. The Endpapers keep written stories and characters safe—or try to. As you know, it doesn't always work very smoothly. Does that make any sense at all?"

"I get the general idea, I think," Tilly said. "I'm not sure any bookwanderers really understand it properly. It is magic after all. Hang on . . ." She stared out the window. "Are we slowing down?"

Milo held on tight to the net of wooden orbs and leaned over to look inside the engine, where the flames were finally losing some of their ferocity and crumbling into glowing embers as the pace of the train started to slow. The flickering images outside the window calmed down and darkened into the sparkling expanse of Story. Tilly peered out of the window and could see nothing but blackness pinpricked with glitter.

"We seem to be just hanging out in the middle of Story," she said, trying to tamp down the feeling of panic that was rising. She felt as though she were lost in space. "But that's okay, right? At least the train feels . . . calmer now."

"*I* don't feel very calm," Milo said, leaning against the wall.

"Let's not forget you worked out how to be the driver," said Tilly. "Or the gist of it, at least. I wonder if it's about having a really clear idea in your head, and we need to actually stop and think about where we want to go to find the cure. We just need a plan—and maybe a hot chocolate?"

Milo gave her a small smile and nodded. *Hot chocolate always helps*, Tilly thought to herself. She followed Milo through to the dining car, which had a small but well-stocked pantry tucked at one end.

"Didn't you use to have a chef?" Tilly asked. She had a memory of someone bringing them food but couldn't remember anything else. Maybe she was getting confused.

"Uh, yeah, I think so," Milo said vaguely. "But we've not had any clients onboard for a little bit, so we don't need one at the moment. Horatio's been fixated on something and even more stressed than usual. He's been getting loads of stuff for that client I told you about, the Botanist."

"Right!" Tilly said, excited. "You said you thought that would be how Horatio would get the cure. So, we should go find this Botanist person!"

"Yes," Milo said. "That's what Horatio said to do before he passed out. He said we need to get the . . . the compendium he called it, and take it to the Botanist. I think. He wasn't being very clear."

"A compendium?" Tilly asked. "What does that even mean?"

"He's looking for this thing he calls a poison compendium, some kind of clever book or box or something that—I'm assuming from the name—has something poisonous inside. He's super focused on getting hold of it, so it must be important. He said he needed it to stop someone, but he didn't have a chance to tell me who before he touched the book. But it was someone he seemed almost scared of? And he's never scared of anyone."

"Do you know where this poison thing is?" Tilly asked.

"Yes, I do know that!" Milo said, pleased. "It's inside *The Wizard of Oz*."

"Okay, well, that's what we do," Tilly said. "We go and get the poison box thingy, and then take it to the Botanist," Tilly said. "Horatio knew Grandad was ill before he arrived at Pages, so maybe he was already looking for the cure."

"He did say that this bad person had other concoctions that he uses to break bookwandering rules, so . . . I guess he and the Botanist are trying to find a way to stop him?"

"There must be something in this poison collection that's the key to it all," Tilly said. "That's why he's so obsessed with finding it. He's on the good side again—he just doesn't like people to know."

"But is any of that safe?" Milo asked. "Going into *The Wizard of Oz*, I mean? And . . . then trying to find someone we don't know? Do we just turn up with this compendium and hope the Botanist knows what to do next?"

"Basically," Tilly said. "And we're way past safe. My grandad and your uncle are unconscious. We have to try and cure them and find out what's going on. There's something bigger happening here, and it's to do with whoever that man is that your uncle seemed frightened about. And we've come this far, right?"

She was trying to stay positive, but the thought of her grandad was constantly in the back of her mind, urging her onward. Even when she and Oskar had been looking for the Archivists to save all of British bookwandering, she hadn't felt as awful as this. This was her *grandad*, the person who had looked after her when her mother had disappeared; the person who read to her in front of the fire every night and learned how to sew name badges on her school uniform; the person who had introduced her to all her favorite stories and who'd walked for hours on Hampstead Heath inventing new ones with her; the person who'd nearly blown up their kitchen by drying her paintings in the microwave, who played board games with her whenever she wanted and who'd first told her she was a bookwanderer.

She couldn't lose him. And so she needed to help Milo feel confident because he was the one with all the clues and the train whistle, and neither of them could do it without each other.

"I thought you were into adventures!" she tried cajoling him.

"I am, in theory!" Milo said. "But I've always been more of a . . . bystander, you know. I like watching other people's adventures or reading about them!"

"Well, this is your own adventure, and it's already started," Tilly said firmly. "So let's go get this compendium thingy and cure Grandad and Horatio—okay?"

"Okay," Milo said. "But hot chocolate first, right?"

"Of course," Tilly said.

21

Not Really a Yes or No Question

O ver mugs of hot chocolate, Tilly heard from Milo everything he knew about the poison compendium and the Botanist, which wasn't that much.

"And Horatio was sure it was inside *The Wizard of Oz*?" Tilly asked.

"Yes, definitely." Milo nodded. "He said it was in a hidden library somewhere in the Emerald City. He said we could get it from *any* copy of *The Wizard of Oz*, that 'he controls them all.'"

"What does that even mean?" Tilly asked. "How can anyone control all the copies of one book?"

"I don't know, but ideally we won't have to bookwander into a book that's poisoned *and* in a language that neither of us speak . . ." He paused. "You don't speak Italian, do you?"

"No." Tilly shook her head.

"Right, well, as I thought, we're not going to get very far in a poisoned Italian copy of *The Wizard of Oz*."

"But, if you can get the poison box from any copy, it must have been hidden in the Source Edition," Tilly pointed out. "And if that's the case, he must own the Source Edition himself so it wasn't impacted when we changed the ones in the British Underlibrary into regular books. That's the only way it makes sense! If you take something into the Source Edition, it would exist in every book, wouldn't it?"

"I think so?" Milo said. "That doesn't seem safe, though. Anyone could get to it."

"But it's so clever," Tilly said, thinking it through. "It means it's easy to access, and you don't need to worry about keeping one particular copy safe. And I've never heard about another bookwanderer who can take something out that they didn't take in, so even if someone found it, they couldn't steal it!"

"Of course," Milo said. "That makes sense of that. Horatio said something about thinking he'd probably invented something to get around it—or that he'd used people to take stuff in, guard them, and then bring them out when he needed them."

"And that's why Horatio needs me, of course," Tilly said. "I suppose this person whose Record we have might be guarding the box for him. What was his name?"

"Theodore Grant," Milo said, showing Tilly the blank

Record. "But that's about all we know. But he's our best bet for finding the poison box, I think."

"If his job is to guard the box, though, might he make things difficult for us?" Tilly said nervously. "I don't think I can fight anyone, just so you know."

"Definitely not," Milo said queasily.

"So your uncle is trying to steal this poison box, or whatever it is, from the man who controls the copies of *The Wizard of Oz*, to take it to this Botanist, who can help stop him?"

"Something like that," Milo said. "But what's it got to do with your grandad? Maybe he knows about all this secret stuff too—through the Underlibrary?"

"Maybe," Tilly said, not liking the idea of more family secrets that had been kept from her.

"And there was nothing in the poisoned book that said where it came from?" he asked. "No explanation?"

"Just this little card with a symbol on it," Tilly said. "It was a circle with a sort of bent line inside it."

Milo froze. "The line—was it like an open book?"

"It could have been, sure," Tilly said. "Or a bird, maybe?"

"Hang on," Milo said, before scurrying out of the dining carriage and returning a few moments later, completely out of breath, with a brown leather book bursting with loose papers. Milo flicked through some of the loose sheets until he found a small rectangular card. He held it up to Tilly.

"Was it this symbol?" he asked breathlessly.

"Yes!" Tilly said. "Exactly the same! What's that you found it in?"

"It's . . . um . . . a family thing," said Milo. "I think."

"Horatio knows so much more than he's told you, or my family, obviously. It's unfortunate that he's so . . . unconscious."

"I'm not sure we'd get any more information out of him if he was awake to be honest," Milo said. "The only time he talked about this was when we got back on the Quip at the shop, after you didn't come with us—he was so stressed out. That's when he mentioned taking the poison box to the Botanist. It's the last thing he said to me."

"And you trust him?"

"That's not really a yes or no question," Milo admitted. "But I can't just leave him like this, and I'm not sure how else we save him and your grandad and work out what's going on without doing what he said."

"Is there anything else that's useful in there?" Tilly asked, pointing at the book Milo had produced the card from. "Should we check the other papers? You said it was a family thing—is it Horatio's too?"

"No, they're mine," Milo said, putting his hand firmly on top of it. "Sorry," he said. "It's family stuff. It's private."

"Okay," Tilly said, trying to suppress her curiosity. "You said . . . you said that you didn't really know any of the rest of your family?"

"Yeah," he said quietly. "But I only just found this. I haven't really had a chance to look at it properly though, with everything that's happened."

"It might make sense for you to look now, if you're comfortable," Tilly said. "If that symbol was in there, there might be more useful information, and we really don't have a lot to go on so far—or much time, if what Horatio said about the poison was true."

Milo nodded, took a deep breath, and opened the book. On the top was the small poster folded in two.

"I don't know what half of the stuff in here is," Milo said, unfolding it. "I saw this earlier, and it's some kind of advert for the Quip, I think, but I'd never heard of Evalina until today."

"'Evalina's Literary Curiosities,'" Tilly read out. "Do you have any idea who she is?"

"I have a theory," he said, searching for a specific photo and holding it out to her. "Look at the back."

Tilly took the photo, which showed Horatio standing with an older woman and a man who was obviously his brother, which would make him Milo's father. On the back it said "Evalina and her boys."

"So . . . Evalina is your grandmother?" Tilly asked.

"I guess so," Milo said despondently.

"When I was on the Quip in the spring, Horatio said that someone used to own the train before him, someone who used it for dinners with book characters and stuff . . . You think it was your grandmother? That certainly sounds like literary curiosities or whatever that poster says. But why didn't he say it was his mum?"

"I've no idea," Milo said. "That's about as far as I'd got working it out. He's so secretive, but I don't understand why he wouldn't have told me that the train is a family business. And, well, where is she now? She can't be much older than your grandparents. I don't even know if she's still alive."

"It probably doesn't help much, but I do know what it feels like to have secrets about your family kept from you," Tilly said. "How do you feel?"

"I feel . . . sad that I don't know anything about my family," Milo replied slowly, "or what happened to my parents, and confused that I might have a grandmother out there somewhere that I don't know about."

"But, Milo," Tilly said, feeling a bit sick, "if your uncle inherited the train, then it's probably quite likely that she's not still around—I'm sorry."

"Well, we don't know that yet," he said. "And it's all I've got. Anyway, there's a load more stuff in here to go through that might tell us where she is. I can look at it all when we're on our way to the Botanist, after we've found the compendium. Then hopefully she can use it to make a cure for your grandad and Horatio, and I can ask him more about it."

"Okay," Tilly said. "You . . . think you can get us to her?"

"Yes," Milo said, sounding way more determined than

Tilly had heard him before. "I've never got off the train, but I've seen where we go when we visit—it's up in Northumberland. I can get us there. I need to know what's going on, and waking Horatio up is the way to work it out. Let's find this poison box."

"So, do you have another copy of *The Wizard of Oz*?" Tilly asked, eyeing the poisoned Italian version that was still lying abandoned under Horatio's desk where it had fallen. "It's all very well saying we don't want to look in there, but do we have another option?"

"I'm sure we do, somewhere," Milo said. "Especially if Horatio knows that it's got something to do with all of this. Let me go look in the library carriage. You look on the shelves in here. I'll be back in a sec."

Tilly had to fight hard to resist the urge to look at the pile of papers from the scrapbook that Milo had left on the desk, but they weren't her secrets to uncover. She started trying the drawers instead, but they were all locked, and Milo had taken the ring of keys with him. She made a mental note to look through them when they got back.

Milo returned a few minutes later holding a satchel and a book, which he held out to Tilly.

"Are you ready?" Tilly said, taking the copy of *The Wizard of Oz*.

"No," Milo said. Tilly looked up at him in surprise. "But we should go anyway," he said weakly. "Where do we read into?"

"Your uncle talked about the Emerald City, right?" Tilly said. "So let's start there." She flicked through the book until she found the right page, linked arms with Milo, who was trembling slightly, and read them in.

> "As they walked on, the green glow became brighter and brighter, and it seemed that at last they were nearing the end of their travels. Yet it was afternoon before they came to the great wall that surrounded the City. It was high and thick and of a bright green color."

22

We're Off to See the Wizard

They had to **squint** as the **dark** wood and copper details of Horatio's office folded down around them to be replaced by bright sunlight glinting off a road made of . . .

"The yellow brick road!" Milo said in delight. "I've never bookwandered in here before, have you?"

Tilly shook her head. The iconic butter-yellow bricks of the road were surreal enough, but the green glow emanating from the wall in front of them was something else.

"The Emerald City!" she whispered in wonder. "Let's go."

The actual city wasn't visible behind the towering wall, only the green haze spilling over the top, like a huge green floodlight pointed upward. As they headed toward it, Milo slipped the book back into his satchel, making sure it was securely closed. As they walked, tuneful chattering drifted on the breeze toward them.

"Look!" Milo said, pointing, and there, coming up behind them, was a very familiar group of travelers.

"Let's wait," Tilly said. "And try and get into the city with them."

"And we need to keep our eyes peeled for anyone that could be Theodore," Milo pointed out. "His Record says he never left the book."

"Do we know anything about what he might look like?" Tilly asked.

"Just that he must be in his early twenties," Milo said, as they reached the group.

"Hello!" Tilly called, and struggled to keep the huge grin off her face as they turned—it was hard not to react to such famous characters. There was a man made of straw with a face drawn crudely on, a shining tin woodcutter with a few scratches from his journey, and a lion who was standing guard in front of the others, shaking slightly. And finally there was a girl about their age in a blue-and-white gingham dress, wearing sparkling silver shoes and holding a small dog in her arms.

"Your shoes aren't red!" Tilly burst out without thinking.

"Why ever would they be?" the girl said in an American accent.

"In the film—" Milo started, but stopped abruptly when Tilly nudged him.

"Sorry, that was a bad start," Milo said, embarrassed, as the four stared at them in utter confusion. "I'm Milo, and this is Tilly."

"How do you do?" the girl said, dipping into a curtsy. "My name is Dorothy Gale, and these are my friends and companions, the Lion, the Tin Woodman, and the Scarecrow. And this is my dog, Toto. We're going to the Emerald City—we're off to see the Wizard—where are you headed?"

"We're going to the Emerald City too," Tilly said. "In search of . . . a lost . . . friend."

"How loyal of you," Dorothy said, a wide and sincere smile on her face. "Let us all go together. Perhaps you should ask the Wizard if he knows your friend? For he is the most powerful and good man in all of Oz."

"He's going to give me some brains," the Scarecrow said.

"And me a heart." The Tin Woodman smiled.

"And courage for me!" the Lion chipped in.

"I hope that he gives you everything you want," Tilly said kindly. "Or that you find it somewhere else if he can't."

"Oh, he will be able to help us straightaway—I am sure of it," Dorothy said. "For he is known to be the wisest magician Oz has ever seen. Why, everyone we have spoken to on our journey here has assured us of it, and I was sent this way by the Good Witch of the North herself!"

"Who else would be able to help us get what we need?" the Tin Woodman pointed out.

Milo and Tilly simply nodded, for it wasn't very polite to point out the error of someone's plan just because you knew the ending.

"So it would be okay if we came with you?" Milo asked. "Just as far as the gate?"

"Why of course," Dorothy said. "I'm always happy to meet new friends."

"Now we must get on," the Scarecrow said. "We have come so far and are so close to the Wizard."

And so the six of them walked up to the imposingly large wooden gate, set with so many emeralds that it sparkled too brightly to look at directly. There was a large, ornate bell hanging by the side of the gate, and Dorothy reached up and pushed the button confidently. A gentle ringing sounded within, and the gates swung open. However, these didn't lead them straight inside the city but into a hall with high, elegant ceilings, also studded with emeralds of all different sizes.

"How much do you think this cost?" Milo said, amazed at the sight.

"Maybe emeralds aren't so expensive here," Tilly said. "Not that I could tell you how much an emerald costs at home. I suppose the Wizard is very rich, even if he is a fraud."

"What did you say?" the Lion asked, whipping round to face them.

And, even though they knew that he was a very kind lion who was much braver than he realized, it was still quite terrifying to have a fully grown lion demanding an answer from you.

"Oh nothing," Milo tried to cover. "Just that the Wizard is so rich and so . . . broad?"

"Broad?" the Lion repeated in confusion.

"Why, yes," Tilly said. "We've heard he has extremely broad shoulders. Haven't you?"

"Of course I have," the Lion said. "And that is only appropriate for such an important man, in my opinion." He gave them another stare before padding back over to stand by Dorothy.

A small door in the wall opened, and out came a very short man dressed entirely in green. He wore a velvet suit the color of moss, a tall top hat in forest green, and pointed shoes in a delicate shade of mint. Even his skin looked slightly green, which made him look a little poorly. He held a large box (green, of course).

"What do you wish in the Emerald City?" he asked the group in an imperious, if slightly squeaky, voice.

"We came here to see the great Oz," Dorothy said politely.

The guard seemed to be anticipating anything but that answer as he sat down on the floor in surprise. Because he was so short, it wasn't very dramatic but undoubtedly not what was expected.

"It has been many years since anyone asked me to see Oz," he said, utterly bemused. "He is powerful and terrible, and if you come on an idle or foolish errand to bother the wise reflections of the Great Wizard, he might be angry and destroy you all in an instant!"

"But we *must* see the Wizard," Dorothy went on, determined. "And we have come an awful long way."

"And it is not a foolish errand, nor an idle one," the

Scarecrow said. "It is of great importance. And we have been told that Oz is a good wizard, however frightening he may be."

"So he is," said the little green man. "And he rules the Emerald City wisely and well. But to those who are not honest, or who approach him out of curiosity, he is most terrible, and few have ever dared ask to see his face."

Dorothy and her friends exchanged anxious looks.

"Our friends wish to see the Wizard," Milo spoke up. "And, in fact, so do we," he added.

Dorothy gave him a grateful smile, but Tilly was worried. "We don't have time!" she hissed. "We have to find the poison box, or Theodore as a backup, and get out!"

"Well, the Wizard might know something. Or he might have seen Theodore, if he's come this way," Milo pointed out. "And, regardless, we need to get inside the city."

"Very well, I will let you proceed," the small man was saying. "Now, I am the Guardian of the Gates, and since you demand to see the Great Oz, I will take you to his palace. But first you must put on the spectacles."

"Why?" Dorothy asked.

"Because, if you did not wear spectacles, the brightness and the glory of the Emerald City would blind you. Even those who live in the city must wear spectacles night and day," the Guardian of the Gates went on. "They are all locked on, for Oz so ordered it when the city was first built, and I have the only key that will unlock them."

"Almost as if he's trying to hide something . . ." Tilly said ominously under her breath.

"What did you say?" the Lion asked.

"Oh, just that . . ." Tilly faltered.

"That he must be trying to . . . guide something," Milo offered.

"Yeah, you know, guide us along. It's very kind," Tilly finished.

"He is a very good and powerful Wizard," the Lion said. "So maybe you are right, and he is helping us along the way to his palace somehow with these spectacles. Perhaps we could not see clearly otherwise."

The Guardian opened the large box he had brought out with him, and they could see that inside lay trays and trays of

spectacles of different sizes and designs, all with green lenses. The Guardian helped fit a pair to Dorothy first, sorting through the collection and picking out a pair with elaborate gold bands instead of arms and gold filigree decorating the frames. He put them over her eyes and then took the two bands and fastened them at the back of her head before securing them with a key he wore on a chain round his neck. Dorothy dealt with it all very politely, as did her companions.

Tilly was impatient to get going, and the Guardian was taking his time selecting the right glasses for each person, but there was nothing else to be done if they wanted to get inside, and so she let him pick out and fasten the glasses to her head. She wished they'd just bookwandered straight inside the city, although they would have stuck out without the glasses, she told herself. The spectacles were rather tight—to stop people being able to slip them off at will, Tilly supposed—but they would deal with having to get them off when they needed to.

That settled, the Guardian put his own glasses back on and, with a great deal of pomp, pushed open a large door in the far wall.

"Welcome to the Emerald City," he said.

23

No Brains at All

The sight was jaw-dropping. A wide street led out from the gate, lined with grand houses all set with emeralds that sparkled in the light. Even the street itself had gems studded into it. There was a neat park of green grass, and jeweled pathways and statues, and even the sun itself looked green from behind the glasses. People bought green lemonade with green pennies and ate green popcorn while dressed in green cloaks. The roads were busy and bustling, and all the citizens were wearing head-to-toe green, as well as the tied-on spectacles.

"Everything isn't really green, is it?" Milo whispered. "It's just because of the glasses, right?"

"I think it must be pretty green without the glasses," Tilly said. "Think of the emeralds in the entrance hall and the Guardian's skin, but these glasses are *definitely* making it greener. Who knows what's really green, and what they just want us to think is?"

"The entrance hall might be just for appearances," Milo said. "Who has this many spare emeralds to put on the ground! It's probably just bits of glass or something."

"Do you think we should make a break for it?" Tilly whispered.

"Maybe," Milo said, looking nervous. "But we don't know where to look. The hidden library could be anywhere—I think trying to find Theodore might be our best bet."

"Okay," Tilly said. "That makes sense. But promise that if we have to wait for ages or it becomes obvious that no one has any idea who Theodore is, we go and look on our own?"

"Promise," Milo agreed.

They stuck closely behind Dorothy as the group followed the Guardian along the winding streets, and the eyes of the citizens of the Emerald City watched them pass. There was no antagonism but plenty of curiosity directed at the parade of three children, a scarecrow, a tin woodman, a lion, and a small dog that followed the man toward the towering building at the center of the city.

"Here are strangers," the Guardian pompously announced when they reached the door of the building. "And they demand to see the Great Oz."

"Step inside," said the pristinely dressed soldier who opened the door. "And I will carry your message to him."

"Good grief," Tilly said. "After all the fuss the Guardian made, that wasn't so hard, was it?"

At this point the Guardian bowed deeply and left them, and

the six of them plus Toto followed the soldier through the palace gates into another large hall filled, of course, with green furniture and green paintings and green-clad servants. There was a large green welcome mat that the soldier insisted they wipe their feet on before he led them in a formal procession to a row of benches.

"Please make yourselves comfortable while I go to the door of the Throne Room and tell the Mighty Oz that you are here," he said, bowing and leaving abruptly.

Dorothy and her friends all turned to look at each other excitedly.

"To think we have traveled this far and finally made it!" Dorothy said. "And soon the Wizard will send me home to Kansas!"

"And give me a brain!" the Scarecrow added.

"And me a heart!" said the Tin Woodman.

"And courage for me!" finished the Lion.

Dorothy turned to Milo and Tilly.

"And he will help you find your friend too," she said kindly. "Is your friend a citizen of Oz?"

"No, a visitor," Milo said. "We actually think he might have been . . . hiding something here."

"How wonderful!" Dorothy said, clapping her hands together. "Treasure and so forth?"

"Some sort of box or container," Milo explained. "Maybe a book of some kind."

"The greatest treasure of all," the Scarecrow said.

"You're very wise for someone with no brains." Tilly smiled.

"It's very kind of you to say, miss," the Scarecrow said. "But I assure you, there are no brains at all in this head of mine! That's why I need the Wizard, after all!"

A few moments later the soldier returned.

"Oh!" Dorothy said. "Have you seen Oz?"

"Oh no," said the soldier. "I have never seen him. But I spoke to him as he sat behind his screen and gave him your message. He said he will grant you an audience, if you so desire; but each one of you must enter his presence alone, and he will admit but one each day. Therefore, as you must remain in the palace for several days, I will have you shown to rooms where you may rest in comfort after your journey."

"Thank you," said Dorothy, as politely as ever despite the delay. "That is very kind of Oz." Tilly was amazed at how unflappable and good-natured she was.

The soldier blew a whistle, and a young woman arrived and bowed in the funny, formal way everyone had here.

"Follow me, and I will show you to your rooms," she said.

Tilly and Milo hung back, not sure what to do.

"Should we go with them or try and speak to the Wizard?" Milo said, looking worried.

"Can we read ourselves forward, to when Dorothy sees the Wizard?" Tilly asked, pulling Milo to one side and letting Dorothy and her friends follow the woman into the palace.

"I suppose . . ." Milo said a little uncertainly. "It's just like fast-forwarding a bit, right? We can't just wander around the palace or the city hoping we stumble across Theodore or a sinister hidden library—we don't know what either of them look like. So I say we try and skip forward."

He slid the book out of the satchel and turned a few pages on from where they currently were, reading them forward in the story. The scene around them blurred and darkened, and then almost immediately, they popped up back in the waiting hall, right in front of Dorothy, who was now wearing a very fancy green dress. Toto had a green ribbon round his neck, which he didn't seem especially pleased by. The maid was there too, looking rather suspiciously at Milo and Tilly.

"Oh hello!" Dorothy said, taking it all in her stride as usual. "Where did you two come from? I am just about to make my request to the Wizard. Would you like to come?"

"The Wizard has said he will only see you one at a time," the maid reminded her.

"Perhaps we can request an allowance just this once?" Dorothy suggested optimistically.

"You're sure you don't mind us coming with you?" Tilly said, taking Dorothy's arm.

"Not at all," she replied kindly.

"I wouldn't test the Wizard's patience today of all days," the maid warned.

"Whyever not?" Dorothy asked. "Is he in a particularly fearsome mood?"

"Indeed, he is," the maid said. "A man was arrested just this morning—a trespasser in the palace! He was caught in the portrait gallery, trying to destroy one of the paintings! It's ever such a to-do, no one knows who he is, and worst of all, he isn't wearing any glasses!"

24 ★

Banished

Tilly exchanged a look with Milo. Surely a trespasser acting suspiciously must be Theodore. Dorothy was watching them carefully, and as the maid left, she spoke quietly to them.

"I do hope it wasn't your friend," she said kindly. "I know you said he had been hiding something."

"At least we know where he is," Tilly said. "Let's hope we can speak to him before the Wizard does anything horrible."

The soldier from the day before came into the waiting hall and spotted them.

"I'm afraid that I need to ask you to wait outside while the prisoner is sentenced," he said. "The Wizard will see you afterward. He is very distressed by the lack of respect and honor shown him by the trespasser and will need to compose himself for a period of time. This way, please."

The three of them followed him into a larger chamber full

of chattering, extravagantly dressed men and women who fell silent when they entered.

"Are you really going to look upon the face of Oz the Terrible?" one woman whispered in awe as they passed.

"Of course," Dorothy said politely. "If he will see me."

"He will see you shortly," a soldier said. "Although, he does not like to have people ask to see him. Indeed, at first he was angry and said I should send you back where you came from. Then he asked what you looked like and, when I mentioned your silver shoes, was very much interested. I am sure you will be granted the great honor of speaking with him once the prisoner is dealt with."

As he finished speaking, a great commotion broke out as the doors to the waiting chamber burst open and two soldiers marched out, holding a man between them. He was very tall, slender, and pale, and no match for the burly soldiers who held him tight.

"Ahem," one of the soldiers said, clearing his throat and puffing his chest out with importance. "Hear ye, hear ye! An announcement from the Wizard! This man has been found guilty of trespassing in the Emerald City and attempting to destroy a painting belonging to the Wizard, as well as contravening several rules that the Wizard, just now, has signed into law."

"What will happen to him?" Milo asked one of the lords.

"Why, he will be punished, I expect," the grand man said, "for daring to affront the Wizard so rudely. An example must be made."

"How do you punish people around here?" Milo asked nervously.

"I'm not at all sure now you come to mention it," the man

said, looking perplexed. "People are usually very well behaved."

The question was answered by the soldier clearing his throat.

"Ahem," he said again. "Because of the charges set against him, and the laws that he has broken, laws our great Wizard has written, because of . . . all of that, and probably much more we don't know about, this man is hereby banished from the Emerald City!"

The prisoner was clearly dismayed by the ruling and started to struggle as he was dragged toward the doors of the palace.

"You must go and see the Wizard now," the friendly soldier said to Dorothy as the three of them watched. "He has composed himself. And, if you do not, you may never again be granted the honor of being in his presence."

"I must go," Dorothy said to Milo and Tilly. "Otherwise, Toto and I shall never get home to Kansas."

"Of course," Tilly said. "I think we're going to stay here and follow this man, though."

"Are we?" Milo said, eyeing up the soldiers.

"It *is* your friend, isn't it?" Dorothy said sadly. "I do hope that you are able to help him find his way home, for there is no place like it."

"And we hope you get everything you ask for," Milo said earnestly.

"Why thank you," Dorothy said, bobbing into a curtsy before smiling warmly and following the soldier into the Wizard's presence.

Milo and Tilly turned their attention to the man, now presumed to be Theodore Grant.

"We need to try and speak to him!" Tilly said. "He doesn't look so dangerous, does he? We must find out if he has the compendium or get him to tell us how to get into the hidden library . . . *and* ask him if he knows what on earth is going on."

They pushed to the front of the crowd, following the soldiers and Theodore along the sparkling streets to the grand gates of the Emerald City. The rest of the gathered people stopped when they reached the entrance hall, as if there were an invisible wall, and Theodore was handed over to the Guardian of the Gates, who seemed most flustered that there weren't any spectacles to remove.

"Oh, but please could you take *ours* off?" Tilly called as they hurried into the hall after the man.

"You wish to leave the Emerald City?" the Guardian said, as though the very idea were preposterous.

"For now, yes," Milo said anxiously as the soldiers escorted the man toward the main gate. "And we're actually in a little bit of a hurry."

"Very well," the Guardian said, taking his time to produce the key that loosened the glasses. "Try not to be too disappointed when you first leave, for everything is so . . . un-green."

"Thank you—we'll try!" Tilly called, and the two of them ran through the gates, only to find the man waiting for them.

"Theodore?" Milo said breathlessly.

"Do call me Theo," the man said in a posh voice. "I assume the Alchemist has sent you?"

25

The Alchemist

"The Alchemist has sent us?" Tilly repeated, confused.

"Hasn't he?" Theo said, taking a step back. "I must admit I was surprised to see him send two children, and neither of them his daughter. But then who are you, and why did you follow me?"

"We . . ." Tilly wasn't sure what to say. She had no idea who the Alchemist was, but then she realized. She glanced at Milo and saw the penny had dropped for him too.

"The 'he' that Horatio kept talking about!" Milo said. Tilly nodded.

"So the Alchemist is your . . ." she started.

"My . . ." Theo paused. "I don't know what you'd call him, really. My employer, I suppose. On a freelance basis."

"And he gave you something to bring here, yes?" Milo asked.

"Yes, he did and . . ." Theo glared at them. "How did you know that?"

"A lucky guess?" Tilly said.

"Well, anyway," Theo said impatiently, clearly preferring to talk about himself and his woes than pay much attention to what two children were doing there as well. "I brought it here for him, to hide and guard until it was needed. And he was supposed to be sending someone to collect me so I could be paid."

"You can't go home by yourself?" Tilly asked in surprise. "Don't you have a book with you so you can read your way out? How long have you been here?"

"Many years," Theo said. "In Oz time, at least, but of course I barely age while I'm here."

"Because of *book magic*?" Tilly asked, and Theo looked at her in confusion again.

"You . . . you don't know the Alchemist's work at all, do you?" he said, starting to sound a little more unsettled. "But then, what are you doing here? How do you know who I am? Where is your copy of the book?" His eyes took on a desperate sheen as they noticed Milo's satchel. "Is it in there? You must give it to me."

"Hang on," Tilly said, trying to think of some way to calm him. "I am sure we can help each other. We can take you out with us if you tell us where the library is hidden—and where the poison compendium is."

"Why would I tell you that?" Theo snorted. "I don't know how you know these things, but clearly you are not one of us. You don't know what you're meddling with. Some free advice from me—get out and hope the Alchemist hasn't already noticed that you're here."

"We can't until we get that poison box," Tilly said. "So you might as well help us if you want us to help you. Or we could just leave you here to wait for this Alchemist man to come and get you, if he ever does," Tilly said. "And we'll find it ourselves. We know you were in the portrait gallery, so it must be there. Let's go, Milo! Bye, Theo, good luck!"

She turned round as if to go back to the city, hoping the risk would pay off.

"No, wait!" Theo said, and Tilly breathed a sigh of relief. "Don't leave me."

"Well, tell us how to get into the library," Tilly said.

"I don't negotiate with children," Theo said dismissively.

"There's no one else here to negotiate with!" Tilly said in frustration. "And we're the only ones who can help you get out! Please. We need that compendium to save my grandad. We have to take it to the Botanist for the cure."

"Oh, *she* sent you, did she?"

"No one sent us!" Milo said. "Obviously there is something big going on, but we don't want anything to do with it! We just want to help our families."

"It's not worth my life to betray the Alchemist to you if you're in league with the Botanist," said Theo.

"Why not?" Milo asked.

"They're archrivals, of course," Theo said, arms crossed petulantly. "You really are in the dark, aren't you? Poor kids. I'd be an idiot to help you steal something from him for her. Like I said, my advice is not to get involved with him, regardless of what he promises you. He probably already knows you're here; he knows everything that happens here. It's his calling card, this book—he has powers here that no one should be able to have."

"His calling card?" Tilly repeated.

"You know, like a token or a symbol. He uses it to show his power, his mastery of *book magic*."

"So if my grandad was sent a poisoned copy of *The Wizard of Oz*, do you think it was from the Alchemist?" Tilly asked.

"Quite possibly." Theo shrugged. "Actually, very likely. And, if it was, then there's no hope of curing him without the Alchemist's help, unluckily for you. He weaves *book magic* into all his poisons; it's not as simple as getting some medicine or asking the Botanist for one of her plants. Only the Alchemist can cure someone he himself has poisoned."

"But we were told by . . . we were told by someone," Milo said, "that if we took this compendium to the Botanist, she'd be able to help."

"Are you sure?" Theo smirked.

"Can you remember exactly what he said?" Tilly asked.

"He said to take the compendium to the Botanist," Milo said firmly.

"But he didn't actually say that the Botanist had the cure?" Tilly pointed out.

"Not in so many words, no," Milo admitted. "But it was implied!"

"I have no idea what your uncle is up to." Tilly sighed.

"I mean, I can see why someone wouldn't send two kids to the Alchemist by themselves," Theo chipped in. "He's incredibly dangerous. You two may have stumbled onto this accidentally, but you're involved now. No adult would pack you off in the Alchemist's direction if they had encountered him before. But, regardless, whoever you're talking about was wrong. The Botanist won't be able to counteract the poison."

Tilly felt ill. They were on some sort of cursed treasure hunt—it was even worse than trying to track down the Archivists. They had no map, and where they were aiming for kept moving.

But before they could decide what to do next, a horrible noise filled the air, making them all press their hands to their ears to try and block it out. Dark shapes appeared in the sky, whooshing toward them in a maelstrom of terrifying cackling, and a repulsive smell like rotting meat filled their nostrils. As they grew closer, the shapes of huge

monkeys became clear, each with a wide, leathery set of wings that flapped them nearer and nearer at a frightening rate.

"The winged monkeys," Theo said, shivering. "I wonder who the Wicked Witch has sent them after this time."

"They're not after . . . us?" Milo stuttered in fear.

"Why would they be after us?" Theo said. "The Witch has no idea who we are. And you know they have to obey whoever has the golden cap—and that's the Wicked Witch. I pity the poor soul she's sent them after, though."

But far from flying over their heads to the Emerald City or further afield, the winged monkeys slowed and landed right in front of the three of them. Tilly felt sick with fear and tried to get Milo's attention so she could signal for him to get the book ready in case they needed to leave quickly.

"What do you beasts want?" Theo said, trying to sound brave, but a quaver in his voice gave him away.

One monkey was considerably larger than the others, and he bounded forward, his tattered wings scraping over the yellow bricks behind him.

"What are your names?" the leader of the monkeys demanded in a scratchy, deep voice.

"Who do you want?" Theo said. "I assure you, it isn't us."

"What are your names?" the leader repeated, stalking even closer so they could see his matted fur and sharp yellow teeth.

"My name is Theodore Grant," Theo started, moving back toward the city gate. "And you do not want me—I am only a visitor to Oz. And I'm under the protection of the Alchemist! And these are . . . Why, I don't even know your names," he said in surprise, looking at Tilly and Milo, who had inched closer and closer to each other.

"Their names do not matter," the leader said. "It is Theodore Grant we have been sent for."

"No, there's been some mistake," Theo said, retreating toward the locked gate of the Emerald City.

"There is no mistake," the leader said, gesturing to his followers.

"But what does the Wicked Witch want with me?" Theo said in horror.

"The Wicked Witch is no longer the owner of the golden cap," the leader said with a leer. "We report to another and owe him his three requests."

"No . . ." Theo said in horror, the truth dawning on him. "He wouldn't." He started pushing desperately at the button that sounded the entrance bell to the Emerald City, but there was no answer.

"Should we try and help him?" Milo whispered, but there was a great horde of winged monkeys between them and Theo now, so they could not even grab hold of him and read him out if they wanted to. Pulling him back from the gate, two monkeys took Theo by an arm each and, flapping their great wings, quickly lifted him up into the air, with no interest in Tilly and Milo.

"He has forsaken me!" Theo shouted in despair from above them. "Find the painting! Look for his symbol!"

He kept shouting, but Tilly and Milo could no longer hear his words, as he was

carried away

by the monkeys

until they were

no more than specks

of black against

the blue sky.

26

A Good Bargaining Tool

Tilly and Milo stared in horror as the winged monkeys shrank away to dots in the sky and then to nothing at all.

"Do you think he'll be okay?" Tilly asked quietly.

"I think it's . . . unlikely," Milo said, looking a little faint.

"If this Alchemist guy is controlling the monkeys now, does that mean he's here?" Tilly said, glancing over her shoulder as if he might appear on the yellow brick road as they spoke.

"Maybe," Milo said. "He clearly has a scary amount of control over the book, though, wherever he is. Theo said he probably knew we were here already, so we need to speed up or at least get out of the open."

"Do you believe him?" Tilly asked.

"About what?"

"That it's the Alchemist we need to find for the cure? Theo

seemed pretty sure that any poisoned copy of *The Wizard of Oz* must have come from him and that he'd be the only person who could give us an antidote."

"I don't see any reason he'd be lying," Milo said. "He didn't exactly come across as a . . . master strategist or anything. He wasn't very good at negotiating. But the last thing Horatio said was that we needed to get the compendium to the Botanist, and that was *after* he'd been poisoned."

"Maybe he was wrong?"

"Maybe. Or maybe the Alchemist is too dangerous?"

"Clearly he's the key to it all, though," Tilly said. "Whatever he is up to is causing all these other problems. And whatever is in this poison box is obviously important, so I still think we need to find it."

"I agree." Milo nodded. "Although I wish I didn't and we could get out of here. It seems that we're going to have to find this Alchemist for the cure, and whatever we find in the hidden library will be a good bargaining tool. I just . . . I don't think Horatio probably was factoring in your grandad's health that much when he told me what to do. And that's the most important thing."

"Thank you," Tilly said. "I can't shake the feeling that Horatio telling us to go to the Botanist was making us cogs in his grand plan. You're right—the only way to wake up Horatio and Grandad and get some answers about how they're involved in all of this is to track down the Alchemist."

"So we need to find this portrait gallery then?" Milo said.

"Back inside the Emerald City," Tilly agreed, and they headed toward the door.

The Guardian of the Gate was most flustered to see them again.

"In and out and in and out!" he said. "But I knew you'd be back; the Emerald City is the most beautiful place in all of Oz! Let me put your spectacles back on." Tilly and Milo begrudgingly allowed the green glasses to be fixed back round their heads and were ushered through the doors onto the gleaming, winding streets of the Emerald City. It didn't take them too long to reach the palace, and they weren't noticed as they entered the outer chamber, where there were still a lot of grandly dressed men and women milling about, watching the doors leading through to the Wizard's chamber.

"Excuse me," Tilly said, tapping an extravagantly dressed woman on the arm. "Do you know where the portrait gallery is?"

"Why, yes, of course, child," the woman said. "It's . . ." She stopped and looked confused. "It's . . . Well, I suppose it's up there somewhere." She gestured vaguely at one end of the hall before turning back to her companions.

"She sounded like she'd forgotten," Milo said.

"I think it's because there's no actual portrait gallery on the page in the book," Tilly said. "It's not in the story, so she's confused. Things that aren't on the page or aren't very well described can get a bit fuzzy, I think. Let's try in this direction—it's somewhere to start."

The two of them climbed a stone spiral staircase from the grand hall up to a floor above. They wandered through corridors laid with green tiled floors, up more stone stairs, through echoey chambers and rooms set with gems, but there were no paintings they could see. There were never any people either, and the rooms were always completely devoid of furniture or details beyond green and emeralds.

Just as they were beginning to lose hope of finding anything that wasn't just a room of emeralds, the corridor made a sharp right turn, and they were no longer in a plain, empty space but a detailed, rich one unlike anything else they'd seen since they'd left the hall. It was furnished properly, with wooden floors, richly embroidered curtains hanging from stained glass windows in different shades of green, and, above all, there were paintings—lots of paintings.

"I think it's safe to say this is the portrait gallery," Milo said, staring ahead at all the canvases.

"How on earth will we know which is the right one?" Tilly said in frustration.

"What did Theo say?" Milo asked. "Find the painting? Look for the symbol? What symbol do you think that is? The one from the poisoned book?"

"Yes. And finding it is another challenge," Tilly replied. "Seeing anything is a nightmare with these stupid glasses on." She yanked at them, but they were firmly locked at the back and closely fitted, and if she tried to pull at them, they only cut painfully into her face.

"Hang on," Milo said, rummaging around in the bottom of his satchel. He pulled out his uncle's ring of keys and sorted through them quickly until he separated out something that wasn't a key. It looked like a Swiss Army Knife with slim metal tools with different delicately curved and spiraled shapes at the ends, similar to but not quite the same as the traditional corkscrew or tiny scissors Tilly had expected.

"Lock picks!" he said triumphantly. "Horatio has all sorts on here for helping him access wherever books are hidden. I should have thought earlier, although I suppose these spectacles do help us blend in. Turn round and let me see if I can do anything."

Tilly span round, and Milo fiddled with the tools until he selected one. She could feel pressure on the back of her head as he inserted the pick into the lock and jiggled it around. It didn't work straightaway, but Milo kept going, trying more of the tools until suddenly . . . *click*! And Tilly felt the spectacles fall loose round her ears.

"You did it!" she said. "That was amazing! But I don't know if I'll be able to do it too."

"Of course you will," Milo said. "We know which tool

it is now, because the Guardian used one key for all of them. I'll talk you through it." He gave her the right tool and turned round. He was taller than her, so she had to stand on tiptoe as he coached her through the sensations she was looking for. He explained the click feeling she was looking for, and quickly she felt that satisfying catch, and Milo's glasses came loose as well.

"Ohhhh," Tilly breathed, as it had suddenly become very obvious which painting stood out. Now the spectacles were gone, they could see that every single portrait in the gallery was painted in shades of green—apart from one.

Tilly and Milo approached the large painting, which showed an old man in blue robes kneeling in front of a glowing glass receptacle, gazing at it in wonder. There was no title or explanation helpfully pinned next to it like in an art gallery or museum, but it *had* to be the one.

"Okay, so what now?" Milo asked. "We're looking for a whole hidden library, aren't we? It must be behind it." He reached forward and tried to pull the heavy frame away from the wall, but it was fastened securely.

"We need to find the symbol Theo talked about," Tilly said, staring closely at the details of the painting. Milo was still poking about the frame.

"I just think," he said, "that in books and stuff, it's always *behind* the painting, isn't it? It's not like we can wander into the painting like we could a book."

They both paused.

"We can't do that, can we?" Tilly said.

"No," Milo said vaguely, and then again more convincingly: "No, we're getting carried away with . . . There's no such thing as traveling inside a painting."

"Right, of course, sorry," Tilly said, and they both privately decided never to mention that conversation again.

"Hang on," Milo said, continuing to inspect the frame and wall. "I think I've found something." The painting was framed in ornate gold, with repeating patterns of fruit, leaves, and decorative curlicues in a rectangle, but molded into it, about level with Tilly's knees, was a circle that was different from the rest of the ornamentation. And across it was a curved line.

"That symbol!" Milo said in excitement. "It *is* the one that came with the poisoned book—and the scrapbook too!"

"You're right!" Tilly said, feeling a flicker of hope come back to life. "You see, it is all connected—it all goes back to the Alchemist. This must be his symbol."

"But why is it in my scrapbook?" asked Milo. "Or being sent to your Grandad?"

"I don't know. But it's why we need to go and find him first. We'll never get any answers, or wake them up, otherwise."

Milo peered in closer, studying the circle.

"So . . . what do we do with it?" she asked.

Milo didn't answer. He tried stroking the symbol and

pushing it to no avail, but then suddenly some particular touch made the whole circle pop upward so it was an inch higher than the rest of the frame. Milo glanced up at Tilly with a grin before twisting it like a wheel.

There was a creaking noise, and then the painting clicked up and swung open, revealing a dark passageway framed by

gold.

27

A Funny Mix of Exciting and Absolutely, Overwhelmingly Terrifying

The passageway disappeared into the **dark**. They could see that it became narrower very quickly, and there was no light at the end of the tunnel. It reminded Tilly of hurtling through the Endpapers; she'd only been there for a few seconds the occasional times she'd traveled that way, but the thought of getting lost there was terrifying.

"Should one of us stay on the outside?" she suggested quietly. "In case it closes behind us?"

"But so long as we can read ourselves out or back in the story, we're okay, right?" Milo pointed out.

"I guess," Tilly said. "But it's really dark in there, and . . ." She tried to think of something to say other than confessing how scared it made her. "I'm just still thinking of those winged monkeys," she finished unconvincingly.

"Okay, well, I'm pretty sure there aren't any winged monkeys in here," Milo said in confusion. "Come on, Tilly. We've got this far. I thought you wanted to find the cure. You're the one who's supposed to be brave, not me. I can't do it if you don't."

"That's not true," Tilly said. "You're just as brave as me. We're maybe just brave about different things." She conjured up the imagine of her grandad, of reading next to him in Pages & Co. "Right," she said, steeling herself. "Let's keep going."

The two of them pulled themselves up into the entrance-way and scrambled along the passage that had been revealed, Tilly leading the way. It was not quite tall enough for them to stand up, so they were forced to crouch or crawl as they felt their way along the cold stone walls, and Tilly could hear the satchel bashing against Milo's hip the whole way down. It was almost entirely pitch-black, with only the faintest glow of light from the hallway they had left behind and no light whatsoever ahead of them. They moved slowly, feeling their way carefully and making sure to put a tentative hand or foot out before moving. Tilly had read far too many adventure books where people fell through trapdoors or down into caverns because they weren't looking where they were going.

After what felt like an eternity of half crawling, Tilly put her hand forward to feel nothing at all.

"There's a drop here," she said back to Milo, carefully feeling all around her. There was nothing—they had reached the end of the passageway. She pulled herself very slowly forward and perched on the side, feet hanging over the edge. Scrabbling around, she found a loose stone, which she dropped over the edge, and felt a huge wave of relief when it clattered to the ground almost immediately.

"I'm going to lower myself down," she said. "I think there's ground just here. Keep hold of my other hand." She felt Milo take hold of one of her wrists, and she gently slid forward, finding that the floor really was very close. She let out a nervous laugh.

"It's barely a drop at all," she said. "Sit on the edge and your feet will almost touch it." She reached back and felt for Milo's hand, helping him find the edge and drop down too.

"At least we can stand upright now," he said.

"Yeah," Tilly said tentatively. "Except it's not much use finding the secret room if we can't see anything in it."

As they spoke, Tilly could hear that their voices had taken on a new tone: there was an echo to their words now they were out of the passageway. And something else was different.

"Can you feel that breeze?" she asked.

"Yes," Milo said. "But I'm mainly just trying not to think about what bugs might live somewhere dark and cold like this."

"I wasn't thinking about it until you said it!" Tilly said.

"Oh sorry," Milo said. "Okay, well . . . just try not . . . to think about it."

"I'm going to have a feel around," Tilly said, trying to be

brave enough for both of them. "If you stay here by the exit and I start moving in one direction and stay touching the wall, we can't lose each other, right?"

There was silence.

"Milo?" she called, panic rising.

"Oh sorry, I nodded," his voice came. "But you can't see me. Sorry. That sounds like a good plan, though, if you're sure. I'll stay here and I can keep talking, and you can find your way back here, whatever happens."

Tilly put both hands on the cold stone wall and started moving them around, inch by inch, very slowly. Almost immediately, she found something sticking out from the side of the wall, also made from stone.

"There's some sort of shelf here," she called.

"Ow! You're still right next to me," Milo said. "No need to shout." And then, at the same moment, the two of them started laughing, and the darkness didn't seem quite so overwhelming as Tilly felt around, trying to work out what she was touching.

"Okay, it's got something on it," Tilly said. "A box? Ohhhh."

"What?" Milo said urgently. "What is it?"

"Hang on," she replied, fumbling with what she had found. "I think if I can just . . . there." And with a scratch and a whoosh and a flare she could see Milo again by the light of a thin taper.

"You could have burned yourself striking that in the dark," Milo said, staying put by the passageway still.

"I think it was worth the risk," Tilly said. She couldn't help but think about all the things she just took in her stride nowadays. She hadn't used to be so brave or so curious, even if she still had some wobbles about the dark. She started to feel as though maybe they were close to working out what was going on and how to save Grandad and Horatio.

"This is almost . . . exciting, isn't it?" Milo said.

"Adventures are a funny mix of exciting and absolutely, overwhelmingly terrifying," Tilly said. "In my experience."

"I'm more used to the terrifying side of things," Milo admitted. "And I'm not sure I've officially even had my own adventure before."

"Your whole life is kind of an adventure," Tilly said, picturing the Quip.

"Not the fun kind," Milo said, and then the taper went out. "Oh bother," Tilly said, fumbling for another one. "Okay, we need to focus and see if there's something else to light," Tilly said. "Surely those matches weren't put there with the intention for you to use them individually." She held the next match up to where the shelf was. A small stone channel came into view, jutting out of the wall right above the shelf that held the matches.

"There's some sort of liquid in there," she said, peering at it before sniffing tentatively. "Can you smell that? It's familiar, somehow. Hang on . . . No, they wouldn't."

"They wouldn't what?" Milo said nervously.

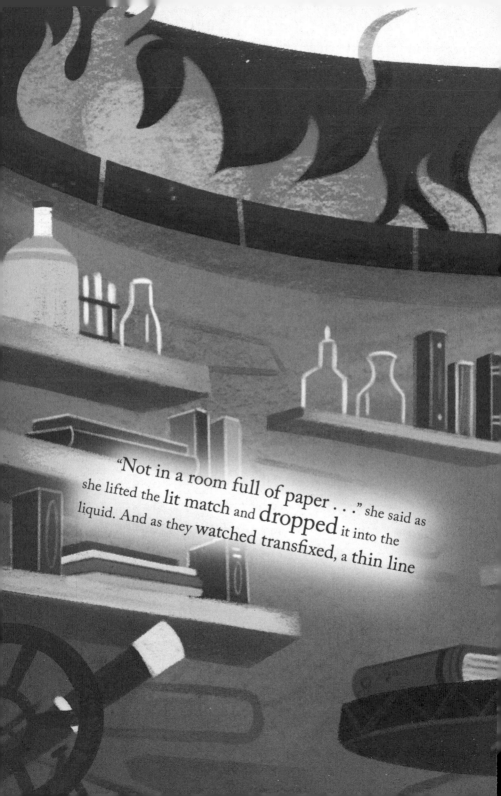

"Not in a room full of paper . . ." she said as she lifted the lit match and dropped it into the liquid. And as they watched transfixed, a thin line

of flame whooshed along the channel, racing in a broad circle that looped round the edge of the room, illuminating the space they were in.

28

Libro del Veleno

As the fire lit everything up, they realized the chamber was much bigger than they had imagined, with shelves made of stone lining the walls. They were filled with books and manuscripts piled on top of each other, glass containers, telescopes, and all sorts of gadgets Tilly couldn't even put a name to. Tilly and Milo stood with their mouths open in amazement.

"Wow," Milo breathed. "That's pretty impressive."

"It's like something out of a film," Tilly said in awe. "Although, why on earth would they light it with *fire* when this place is full of paper?"

"Because it's cool," Milo said, as if that were obvious.

"But how is it staying lit without any air?" Tilly asked, wracking her brains for what they'd learned at school about fire. "It needs heat, fuel, and air to burn, right? So, the matches are the heat, and whatever's in that channel is the fuel, but there's no air—is it going to go out soon?"

"There's that breeze coming from somewhere," Milo reminded her. "But we don't know how long we've got. Maybe it's like a timer with—just enough air to keep the fire lit in order to put something in or take something away—and to put off intruders."

"Well, let's hurry up," Tilly said. "We definitely don't want any company. But how on earth do we find the poisons in here? This place is humongous."

The chamber was large and full and not organized in any obvious order. Papers and books heaped up with gadgets, charts and scientific-looking equipment all pushed together higgledy-piggledy, with more piles on the stone floor.

"Okay, what do we know about this poison compendium?" Tilly said. "I don't really even know what that word means. All we know is it has to be able to hold poisons, right?"

"Horatio said that he wasn't sure exactly what it would be," Milo said. "A box or a book, I think he said—but I don't think it's going to be huge."

"Well, there's nothing else to do but to just start looking and hope it becomes obvious," Tilly said. "If we begin at the passage entrance and work around the walls in opposite directions, we'll meet in the middle. Shout if you see anything that even might be it."

The two of them started trying to sort through the shelves methodically, ignoring the stacks of papers and examining the boxes and gadgets and larger books. As Tilly searched, she realized a lot of the papers and letters and books weren't in English. Some were in what she thought might be Latin, but there were also things in what appeared to be Chinese—and other alphabets she didn't recognize at all. Despite the urgency of the task, it was hard not to get distracted by the weird and wonderful books gathered here, although this was pierced through by an annoyance that this Alchemist man was hoarding it all for himself. Even if he hadn't been a power-hungry poisoner, Tilly wouldn't have liked him after this.

She was interrupted from thoughts of her ever-increasing vendetta against the Alchemist by a grunt and a crash. She looked over her shoulder to see a huge pile of papers fluttering to the floor round Milo's feet.

"Oops," he said sheepishly.

"What happened?" Tilly asked.

"I was just moving this book to look behind it, but it was way heavier than I was expecting, and it threw me off balance," Milo said, gesturing to a large, old book, bound in cracked ruby leather. He heaved it off the shelf and looked at the cover.

"*Libro . . . del . . . veleno,*" he sounded out. "I wonder what that means. Sounds like Latin or Italian, maybe? 'Libro' means book, I'm pretty sure, but I don't know what the rest of it says."

"Me neither," Tilly said, coming to look. "Is that a . . . skeleton on the cover? Creepy. I wonder what it's about."

"It's locked, whatever it is," Milo said, showing Tilly that the book was held together by two large metal clasps on its side.

"You could try your lock pick again, but I'm not sure we have time to look at—"

"It's not real," Milo interrupted her.

"What?"

"It's not a real book; these aren't real pages," Milo said in excitement, touching the edges. "Look, it's wood marked to seem like pages." He ran a finger down the side of the cover and found a catch, which he clicked open. The front swung outward to reveal around twenty tiny wooden drawers, each marked with a paper label that looked like more Latin. There were also gaps between the drawers where minuscule glass bottles were secured with cords. Another drawing of a skeleton was on the inside front cover, and a small skull was emblazoned over the top of the drawers.

"I think we've found it," Tilly breathed. "The poison library. Be careful," she said as Milo stood the wooden library on its base so the drawers were the right way up. "We don't know what any of these are."

Milo very gently eased open one of the drawers, and it was full of dark, dried berries. He peered at the label.

"*Atropa belladonna*," he spelled out. "Have you heard of that?"

Tilly shook her head. They gently opened some of the other drawers and found more berries, as well as leaves, powders, and dried flowers, all with scientific-sounding names on the labels. Some of the bottles were empty, but some were sloshing with different-colored liquids, and they didn't risk trying to unstopper them.

"We've found it," Tilly said again. "I can't believe it. Now we just have to work out what to do with it."

The fire in the channel started sputtering, and they glanced up to see that the flames were starting to weaken and dim.

"It's time to go, I think," Milo said. "At least we have one more piece to the puzzle and a bargaining tool. Maybe the Alchemist will trade it for the cure? Whatever we do, we should get back to the Quip first, before the fire goes out."

Milo pulled *The Wizard of Oz* from his satchel and flicked to the end of the book while Tilly carefully fastened the poison book shut and heaved it up into her arms. Tucking his hand into her elbow, Milo found the last line and read them out.

"And oh, Aunt Em, I'm so glad to be at home again!"

MILO

29

Evalina's Literary Curiosities

Milo was not sure he'd ever felt happier to be back onboard the Quip. He took in the reassuringly familiar scent of *book magic* and smoke as Tilly heaved the poison cabinet onto his uncle's desk. They sat down on opposite sides of the desk and both breathed a sigh of relief.

"So . . ." Tilly started but tailed off.

"So," Milo continued. "Where do we find the Alchemist?"

"It must say somewhere in here," Tilly said, gesturing at Horatio's desk and shelves. "We can work it out."

Milo paused. His idea of his uncle was becoming all muddled; Horatio had saved him by not letting him touch the book and had given him the whistle when he went into Theo's Record, but because his uncle had never shared anything with him until it was almost too late, it was hard to trust any of it. He was clearly involved in something dangerous, which Tilly's grandad had somehow been caught up in too. And leaving aside the big picture, the fact remained that the only person Milo was likely to get answers from about his family—and the scrapbook—was Horatio.

"Okay," Milo nodded. "Let's see if we can find where the Alchemist is. And if we can't?"

"I guess we take the poisons to the Botanist," Tilly said. "But it seems unlikely there won't be some sort of clue if the Alchemist is the key to all of this. Horatio either knows him or knows a lot about him."

Milo pulled Horatio's ring of keys from his satchel and tried a few until he managed to get the desk drawers open. Inside were several large ledgers, labeled on their sides.

"Passenger log, client queries and requests, client information, Bookmarks," he read out loud.

"Client information seems a sensible place to start," Tilly said, and held out her hand for it. "Did you . . . did you want to look at your scrapbook again as well? The Alchemist's symbol was in there after all—there might be more information."

Milo had avoided thinking about the scrapbook for most of the time that they were bookwandering inside *The Wizard of Oz*, but he knew Tilly was right. She was studiously focused on the ledgers, and he appreciated that she was giving him some privacy. He tried to steady his breathing and picked up the scrapbook. This was important and he needed to be useful, not just for himself but for Tilly and her family.

Milo thought of Bobbie, staying strong for her siblings in *The*

Railway Children, and began. He found newspaper cuttings from real newspapers that had no idea about bookwandering, reviewing "Evalina's Literary Curiosities"—his grandmother seemed to have used the Quip to create unnervingly realistic events and encounters for non-bookwanderers. From what Milo could gather, the newspapers had decided that particularly convincing actors must have been hired to play famous fictional characters.

There were letters back and forth with the Marters, in which Horatio asked—apparently regularly—for details about how Milo was doing and also requested lists of visitors to their house. And then there was that folded letter, the one on the thick creamy paper with the broken wax seal. Peering closer, Milo felt his skin prickle with realization as he saw that stamped into the wax was the Alchemist's symbol.

He lifted the cracked wax and read.

AGREEMENT BETWEEN MR. HORATIO BOLT
(The Driver)
AND MR. GERONIMO DELLA PORTA
(The Alchemist)

This agreement states that in exchange for the preservation of his life, the ownership of the Sesquipedalian (the Train) shall pass from the Driver to the Alchemist upon the Driver's death or retirement, subject to the below terms.

The Driver hereby states that he has no living relatives who might inherit the Train and is free to bequeath it to the Alchemist.

The Driver will also agree to source and retrieve manuscripts, books, and other items at the request of the Alchemist, subject to appropriate payment. The Driver is free to accept commissions from other clients, so long as they are not in conflict of interest with the Alchemist's requirements and the Driver provides records of said commissions on a monthly basis.

The Driver's life, preserved only by the actions of the Alchemist, will be surety against this agreement, and the breaking of any of the above terms will require that life to be forfeit.

Signed,

Geronimo della Porta

Horatio Bolt

30

Comfort Blanket Books

Milo dropped the piece of paper, his heart thumping hard. His uncle had sold the Quip to the Alchemist? In exchange for his life? Why did the contract say that Horatio had no living relatives? What was going on?

His spiraling thoughts were interrupted by a frustrated noise from Tilly. "I suppose he has another name, a proper name," she said. "There's no mention of an Alchemist anywhere."

"Try Geronimo della Porta," Milo said quietly.

"Huh?" Tilly queried. "Why?"

"Just have a look," Milo said.

There was silence apart from Tilly turning the pages.

"I've got him," she said. "It looks like he lives in . . . Venice! Wow, I've always wanted to go there. How did you know to check that name?"

He just passed her the contract and watched as her face went from curiosity to confusion to distress.

"You didn't know about this?" she asked.

"Of course not!" he said. "I hadn't even heard of the Alchemist until Theo mentioned him!" He started to breathe very quickly, feeling as though he couldn't quite catch his breath. "I just need a minute," he said, and scrambled out of his chair, out the door, up the ladder, and onto the top of the Quip.

Milo lay on the top of the carriage and stared into the expanse of Story. It was so vast and so beautiful, and it always made him feel calmer to look up at it. His breathing started to slow as he let its tranquility wash over him.

"Milo?" a quiet voice came floating up. "Are you okay? Shall I leave you be?"

"You can come up," he said back to Tilly, only just loud enough for her to hear. Tilly's footsteps clanged on the ladder rungs as she climbed up to the roof.

"Do you want to talk about the contract?" Tilly said.

"Not at the moment."

"Okay," Tilly said, and he heard her lay down next to him.

"It's incredible, isn't it?" he said, gesturing up at the blackness after they had lain there quietly for a moment.

"It's beautiful, but it's so big," she replied. "Don't you find it overwhelming?"

"Never," he said. "It makes me feel like I'm part of some bigger story."

"I like that," Tilly said. "That's a good way of looking at

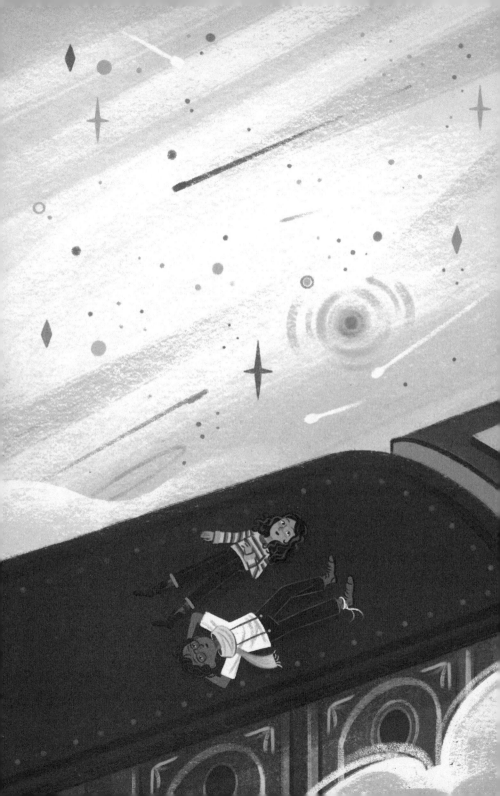

it. I feel like that when I'm reading—not even when I'm book-wandering, just regular reading."

"You said that thing still happens to you sometimes?" Milo asked. "When stories start spilling out of books?"

"Occasionally," Tilly admitted. "We're not quite sure if it's because so many of the Source Editions have been freed and turned into normal books, or what. Also, I'm more alert to it happening, and I can stop reading as soon as I feel it starting. Sometimes it makes me miss just normal reading, you know, before I knew I was a bookwanderer."

"I never really had that," Milo said. "I've always known about bookwandering, for as long as I can remember, because it's why my parents died."

"They died in a book?"

"I guess so," Milo said. "No one knows the details, or at least no one's ever told me. But all the kids at the Marters were there because of bookwandering—because what had happened was too difficult to explain to schools and social workers and stuff. I was too little to actually bookwander by myself at the time and Horatio doesn't really encourage it, so I read normally a lot, but I've always known there was all this magic lurking behind the pages."

"My grandad would say there's magic lurking behind the pages regardless of whether you're a bookwanderer or not," Tilly said, and Milo heard her sniff and wipe her eyes roughly with her hand. "I'm so scared that I won't be able to help wake him up. Amelia has been doing all this research at the Underlibrary, but it seems like there's only one person who will be able to help, and it's the person who did it in the first place. I wish I could ask Grandad's advice and ask him why he's mixed up in all of this." She gave a small, sad laugh. "Do you know who the other person I wish we could ask is?"

"Who?" Milo asked.

"Anne Shirley." Tilly smiled. "You know how some people have comfort blankets or toys? *Anne of Green Gables* is my comfort blanket book. I've read it so many times and it always makes me feel braver."

"Mine's *The Railway Children*," Milo said. "I bookwander there so much." He was surprised that he didn't feel at all embarrassed sharing this with Tilly. "I always think about what Bobbie would do when I'm feeling scared or lonely."

"Anne pops up sometimes at home—at Pages & Co.," Tilly said. "She always seems to turn up when I need her. Do characters do that here?"

"Not without Horatio going and getting them," Milo said. "I guess we're moving about too much. I wish the Railway Children would visit—I bet they'd love the Quip. But don't you find it hard that Anne doesn't remember you every time?"

"Oh," Tilly said, a little awkwardly. "She does remember me. It's to do with me being half-fictional. None of the rules work properly on me, you know, like the whole stories-leaking-out-of-books thing."

"Wow," Milo said, struggling to suppress his immediate feeling of jealousy. If only Bobbie, Peter, and Phyllis could remember him every time he visited.

"But I'm the unusual one," Tilly said hurriedly. "And you still get to go inside *The Railway Children*—something most readers can only dream of."

"I suppose," Milo said. "I sometimes feel . . . This sounds silly, especially as they have no idea who I am, but I feel like they're my brother and sisters. I just know them so well."

"That's why all reading is magical in some way. Grandad . . ." She paused, and Milo heard a wobble in her breath before she went on. "Grandad always says that the books we read help us choose who we want to be, that we're all made up of the characters that mean something to us."

"I guess we're all built of stories," Milo said. "It makes me think of the Records at the Archive—the way they show the books that make someone who they are. I wonder what it looked like when Horatio traveled inside one. I imagine it like a big library full of every book we've read."

"If someone could look at a big list of all the books I've ever read, it would be like reading my diary, wouldn't it?" Tilly mused. "You could tell a lot about someone from what they read, I reckon—who they are. I bet the Alchemist's comfort blanket character is someone like . . . like Miss Trunchbull or . . ."

"Or the White Witch!" Milo suggested.

"Or the Grinch!" Tilly added, and they kept suggesting the most villainous, horrible characters they could think of until they were laughing instead of worrying.

"I'm glad you're here," Milo said.

"Me too," Tilly said. "Thank you for helping me."

"Shall we go and find him then?" Milo said, sitting up and feeling braver. "This Alchemist? Let's go get the cure."

31

L'alchimista

The pieces had started slotting together a little more for Milo now that they knew the Alchemist lived in Venice. Horatio had taken the Quip there several times, even though Milo had never been allowed off the train. So, despite the fact that there wasn't a specific address in the ledger, he was confident he could imagine the canal they always stopped on perfectly, which should be enough to get them there.

This time, the journey was much calmer. They kept the engine topped up with *book magic*, and the Quip slid smoothly through the inky dusk of Story until it slowed to a gentle stop around an hour later. Milo opened the door onto warm evening air, the smell of coffee, and the sound of lapping water.

The train was squeezed in between two streets of tall, slender buildings, some of crumbling brick and some painted in warm yellows and oranges. One side had a narrow pathway that ran alongside the edge of the canal; the other dipped straight into the water, dark apart from the reflection of the lanterns hung above the pathway. Just ahead of them was a narrow, arched stone bridge that stretched from the path to a gap in the houses on the other side, and on the water were a few small, colorful boats tied to hooks on the wall.

"And you're *sure* people can't see us?" Tilly asked nervously.

"People never notice what they don't want to." Milo shrugged. "You have to be able to imagine something is possible to be able to see it, and most people just can't even imagine a scenario where there's a train parked on . . ." He peered out to confirm. "On a canal."

"We're *on* a canal," Tilly said queasily.

"Yep," Milo said, feeling proud of the Quip's cleverness. "I mean we're not floating on it—we're in the space above it, so we can't sink or anything like that."

The two of them looked out, and even though Milo was trying to seem confident in front of Tilly, he'd never been in charge of parking the Quip before and was worried there actually might be some kind of cloaking device or something that Horatio used to keep it hidden from view. He gathered up a copy of *The Wizard of Oz* and one of the Alchemist's business cards, along with a notebook and pen, and opened the door.

The path was empty, there was a chill in the air, and Milo realized he had no idea what time it was. It must be very late or early, given that they'd left Pages & Co. around midnight. He glanced around, but all was still and quiet, only the echo of revelries from somewhere else in the city breaking the silence. He was about to wave Tilly forward when he saw something across the street: a pale face staring right at him.

"Can you see that?" he asked, grabbing Tilly's arm.

"Ow! What?" she said, peering out.

"The face—I think it's a girl," he said, pointing to where he had seen the face, but it had already vanished into the gloom.

"Do you know where to go from here then?" Tilly asked, as they hopped off the Quip and onto the path.

"Not really," Milo admitted. It all felt very familiar to him—this was definitely where Horatio left the Quip when they visited Venice, but Milo had never ventured into the streets before, and he wished he'd paid more attention to the direction his uncle disappeared off to. He patted the whistle to make sure it was safe under his jumper and locked the carriage door carefully, adding the ring of keys to his satchel. The sense of confidence he'd had when he and Tilly had been on top of the Quip was quickly vanishing now that they were in the back streets of a strange city late at night.

"Well, if you were some kind of evil alchemist, where would you live?" Tilly said, staring up at the tall buildings.

Milo looked around them again, desperately hoping there

was something that would trigger some sort of memory that would point them in the right direction, but nothing came to him.

"Okay, well, let's just keep walking," Tilly said. "And look for the symbol or anything to do with *The Wizard of Oz*. But we need to not get lost—let's stay close to the Quip and not go round too many corners. Or we could always turn left."

"Huh?"

"That's what you're supposed to do in a maze, isn't it?" Tilly said. "Always turn left."

"That doesn't sound quite right," Milo said. "At all. Let's draw a map as we go. I've got a notepad."

"Fine," Tilly said. "But I'm sure that maze thing is real. I read it somewhere."

They headed up one of the alleyways at random, and Milo marked the name of it on his map, copying down the Italian words letter for letter to make sure it was accurate. They kept walking, Milo drawing lines and writing down names as they went. It was clearly not a very touristy corner of the city, and they didn't pass much that was open apart from the odd little bistro spilling out onto the street where everyone they heard was speaking Italian. Milo was starting to give up hope of them finding anything, including probably the way back to the Quip, when they passed a bookshop. It was closed, but there were lights on inside, despite the late hour.

"Shall we ask them if they know?" Tilly suggested.

"Booksellers are pretty likely to be bookwanderers, so they might have an idea."

"Even though it's so late?" Milo said, not wanting to cause anyone any bother.

"But they're still up if there are lights on—I think it's worth a try," Tilly said, and walked up to the bookshop. They could see a middle-aged woman drinking from a steaming mug and reading a book under the warm glow of a lamp. Tilly knocked gently on the window, and the woman jumped.

"*Siamo chiusi!*" she called, shaking her head. Seeing their confusion, she stood up and came to the door. "I am closed. It is very late," she said in English before seeming to realize that they were children. "Do you need help?"

"Yes," Milo said. "Please."

"What has happened?" She looked very worried. "Do you want me to telephone the police?"

"Oh no, nothing like that," Tilly jumped in. "We're fine. We're just looking for someone."

"Your parents?" the woman said. "What are you doing out so late? It is not safe!"

"We didn't realize it had got so late—we're sorry," Milo said.

"But we do need help," Tilly said. "It's to do with books."

"With magic books," Milo said.

"Ah. You are . . ." The woman paused, looking for the word.

"*Voi siete le librovaghe* . . . I do not know the word in English."

"We're bookwanderers," Milo said. "You too?"

"*Sì*," the woman said, but this did not seem to reassure her. "Who are you looking for?"

Milo opened his satchel and pulled out the card with the Alchemist's symbol on it. He showed it to the woman, who instantly turned pale and backed away.

"*L'alchimista*," she said under her breath. "Why do you have this?"

"We need to find him," Milo said.

"He is very dangerous," the woman said. "Adults would not seek him out, and you are only children. I cannot help you—I am sorry."

And she swung the door closed.

32

Poison on the Water

"**W**ait!" said Milo, panicking and shoving his foot forward, where the door promptly slammed onto it. "Ow!" he yelped. "That never looks so painful in films."

"I am truly sorry." The woman frowned. "But . . ."

"Please," Milo cut her off in desperation.

"The Alchemist," Tilly added. "He has something we need to save my grandad. And Milo's uncle."

"They are . . . sick?"

"Yes—poisoned," Milo said.

The woman did not even seem particularly surprised. "And you believe he knows the only way to cure them?"

They nodded. The woman looked ill at ease, unsure of whether to help them. But she didn't try to close the door on them again.

"He is at number seventeen," she sighed eventually. "Two

streets from here. Look for the number and the symbol. There is a sign, but it is in Italian. Do you have somewhere I can write it down?"

Milo passed her the piece of paper with his hastily drawn map on it, which made her smile. She drew a few extra lines and marked the place with a star. Next to it she wrote *"Cicuta sull'acqua."*

"What does that mean?" Tilly asked.

"I do not know the English word, but *cicuta* is a type of poisonous plant, and *sull'acqua* means on the water—as we are in Venice, I suppose."

"So . . . poison on the water," Milo said nervously. The woman nodded and retreated back into her shop, pointing in the direction they should go.

"In bocca al lupo," she said, closing the door and locking it behind her.

Milo and Tilly looked at each other anxiously.

"Well, the good news is we know where to go," Tilly offered.

"I guess we shouldn't be surprised that people would have that reaction." Milo swallowed nervously. "We know he's dangerous. And it is the middle of the night after all."

The bookseller's map translated easily into real life, and after only a few minutes' walk they found themselves in a wider, grander avenue than the one they'd come from. Milo realized that he'd been expecting something darker and creepier, more suited to a man who was poisoning people and striking terror into the hearts of neighborhood booksellers. In fact, the street was distinctly well-to-do, with neatly kept window baskets and lanterns. Everything looked very respectable.

Milo and Tilly walked along the empty street until they reached number seventeen. The house was just as neat and grand as the others. Seventeen was marked in brass numbers on the wall, which was painted a rich terra-cotta color. Flowers decorated several balconies, and a warm yellow lantern hung over the wooden door. An easy-to-read sign spelled out *Cicuta sull'acqua*. It attracted no undue attention and did not stand out. Milo thought that the name could mean anything at all to passersby; if this really was the right place, then it was hidden in plain sight from anyone who did not know what they were looking for.

There was a bell with a rope pull on the other side of the door from the numbers. Milo exchanged a glance with Tilly and reached up to yank it. They could hear it echoing within the house, and despite the late hour, after only a few moments, the door creaked open. Again, their expectations were upended. Instead of a dark corridor and strange smells and sights, there was a brightly lit hallway. Warmth emanated from it, as well as the smell of something sweet and rich. A man with white hair, wearing a neat dark suit, held the door open and nodded his head to them but didn't say anything.

"We're here to see the Alchemist," Milo said, trying to sound confident.

The man nodded again, stood back to let them in, and then closed the heavy door behind them.

The sweet smell only intensified as they entered the hall, which was wonderfully, comfortingly cozy. Milo and Tilly let the warmth get into their bones, realizing how cold they had become as they'd walked. The hall had a high ceiling and was painted a beautiful teal color. It was hung with paintings of men and women in different historical dress; some looked very old and some much more modern. A sweeping staircase led off from one side of the hall, and an archway was set into the other. This was where the old man led them, in silence.

They followed him without speaking, their footsteps first echoing on the shining wooden floors and then absorbed by thick carpets. The archway opened onto another lavishly decorated room, with more paintings and plush rugs. A fire roared in a grand hearth, and they could see the silhouette of a man sitting on a sofa staring into its flames. As they entered the room, he turned slowly and smiled.

"Mr. Bolt and Ms. Pages, I presume," he said in perfect English with a strong Italian accent. "Welcome to Venice. Come, sit. You have not come the way I expected you to, but I am very pleased to meet you nonetheless."

33

There's Always Room for a Little Whimsy

Milo was expecting someone who looked more obviously . . . well, evil. It was hard to tell how old the man by the fire was; he had gray hair and a neat gray beard but unlined, tanned skin, and he moved with the ease of a very young person. He was dressed finely but not ostentatiously: an expensive-looking burgundy wool jumper over a crisp white shirt, gray trousers with a sharp line down the front, and shiny black shoes. He saw them taking him in and laughed.

"You were expecting, what, a supervillain in a costume?" he said, and Milo blushed. "I keep my cape for special occasions. Now, Tommaso, please bring us some spiced biscuits and coffee. Do you drink coffee?" He didn't wait for their answer. "Now, come and sit here." Milo and Tilly paused, the warmth of the welcome still confusing them. "I said, come and sit here," the

Alchemist repeated firmly. "Surely you have not come all this way to stare at me from the door."

He was right, and so Milo and Tilly walked over to the fire, glad of its warmth, and sat on the sofa opposite the man, who laid his hands open at them.

"So," he started. "Here you are. Both of you."

"You're the Alchemist?" Milo asked.

"Indeed," the man replied. "I do have a more traditional name, but I enjoy the sense of grandeur and reputation a moniker like that adds. There's always room for a little whimsy."

"Do you study alchemy then?" Tilly said. "Is that where the name comes from?"

"A good question," he replied. "And yes, I have studied it extensively. But I am curious as to what you two know about the subject."

"Is it something to do with the philosopher's stone?" Tilly said.

"I thought it was to do with turning things into gold." Milo added.

"You are both right," the man said. "Many students of alchemy who have gone before me were interested in precisely those things; they studied the elements of our world and how a great mastery of them can lead to progress. They tried to make base elements into precious ones and to preserve and extend human life. But there was one element that long eluded and bewitched them—something that has been called aether, or quintessence, or sometimes even the fifth element. Plato called it the most translucent kind of air, and the ancient Greeks thought it to be the very essence that the gods breathed. Nowadays it is dismissed as a word for something and nothing, but it is not: it is the basis for the very building blocks of our world. It is indeed the substance that fills the air and the universe, the medium light can travel through and the way the light gets in. And this is what all my work is rooted in. I wonder, have either of you worked out what I speak of?"

"Imagination," Milo whispered.

"Precisely." The Alchemist smiled. "You pay more attention

than your uncle gives you credit for. And, speaking of that gentleman, is he not with you?"

Milo was thrown; the Alchemist seemed to know so much and yet not what had happened to Horatio.

"He's ill," Milo said tentatively. "Because of . . ." He stopped, not wanting to give away one of the few things the Alchemist didn't seem to know already.

"Because of the poisoned book," Tilly said fiercely, apparently not so concerned. "That *you* sent. We've come for the cure. And I want to know why you sent it to my grandad. What's he got to do with all of this?"

"Very little, Matilda," the Alchemist said. "I wish him no ill will."

"But you *poisoned* him," Tilly said in disbelief.

"I did," the Alchemist said. "Temporarily."

At this point the old man called Tommaso returned and set down a tray filled with small cups of strong coffee and a china plate heaped with delicate biscuits. They smelled

amazing, but Milo knew it wasn't wise to eat or drink anything that came from the kitchen of a morally dubious alchemist. He watched Tilly work through a similar temptation before declining the plate.

The Alchemist calmly picked up a cup and sipped his coffee elegantly. He had the aura of a man who never burned his tongue on hot drinks.

"You haven't told us why you poisoned my grandad!" Tilly said. "You can't distract us with biscuits!"

"I can but apologize," the Alchemist stepped in. "That was not my intention. Only, you have traveled a long way, by yourselves, it is very late, and you must be very tired—and hungry, no? Assuming that your method of transport is safely stowed, I propose that we have a late supper and then we can discuss matters further. What do you say?"

Milo saw the panic on Tilly's face, and he knew she was thinking about her family and how much they would worry once they woke up and noticed Tilly had vanished. He wasn't sure there was anyone who would even notice if he never returned from Venice. No one awake anyway.

"Do you have a phone I could use?" Tilly asked.

"Who do you need to contact?" the Alchemist responded.

"I need to tell my grandma and my mum that I'm safe," she said. "Obviously," she added under her breath. The Alchemist gestured to Tommaso, who brought over a small notepad and an elegant fountain pen.

"If you write a message for them here, Tommaso will ensure they get it."

Tilly looked unconvinced but did as she was asked, and Milo wondered what she had written.

"I'd like to speak to them on the phone as well," she said, determined.

"Excellent," the Alchemist said. "But it is very late, so perhaps after some food? If you'll—" He broke off and flicked his head toward the archway. "Alessia!" he shouted sharply. "Is that you?"

Round the corner popped a pale face—and Milo realized with a jolt that it was the face that had spotted them when they first arrived.

34

A Point of Principle

The girl moved forward into the light of the room. She had very straight blond hair and was wearing navy-blue silk pajamas under a brocade dressing gown and velvet slippers on her feet.

"What do you think you're doing?" the Alchemist said coldly in English, and the girl responded in a torrent of Italian. "Do not be so rude—speak English in front of our guests," the Alchemist added.

"I am not *doing* anything," she said in flawless English with a far less pronounced accent than the Alchemist. "I was just passing on the way to the kitchen."

"Do not lie to me," the Alchemist said. "You are not invited to supper. Get back up to bed now and stop eavesdropping. Tommaso can get you water if you need it."

The girl shrugged and didn't say anything else. And then, quick as a flash, as soon as the Alchemist had turned round, she winked at Milo and darted back out the room.

"I do apologize for my daughter," the Alchemist said with no further explanation. "Now, if you'll follow me." He stood gracefully and gestured down the corridor. There wasn't much else to do but agree, and Milo tried to ignore the feeling that they had walked right into the lion's den by choice. They were taken into a long room with a dark wooden table in its center, somehow already laid for three people. The Alchemist pulled out chairs for Milo and Tilly before seating himself at the head of the table.

"How is this all ready?" Tilly asked.

"I do not keep usual hours," the Alchemist replied. "Please do not worry that I am up at this time for your benefit. I am older than I look and do not need so much sleep anymore."

A woman in a black dress and white apron quietly set a glass of red wine in front of the Alchemist and two glasses of water in front of Milo and Tilly.

"I assure you all the food and drink is quite safe," the Alchemist said. "I saw that you avoided the biscuits and coffee. I am very interested to meet both of you and would not have brought you here just to poison you with a biscuit."

"You didn't bring us here," Tilly said. "We came by ourselves."

"As I said, you did not arrive as I was expecting, but—and I am sorry to disillusion you—I required you both. The book sent to your grandad, it was more of an invitation than a gift."

"I don't understand," Tilly said.

"While I do not wish your grandfather any ill will, Matilda, I did need you to have a reason to come here, with Horatio, who I had thought was my right-hand man in executing this plan."

"My uncle was in on this?" Milo said, struggling to keep everything straight.

"Of course," the Alchemist said, as easily as if he were explaining a recipe to them. "He does not know as much as he believes he does, but he knew I needed you, Matilda, and he knew my plan for getting you here. I did not think it was likely you would answer a more traditional invitation, and so I created an incentive. Your grandfather would fall ill, and Horatio would arrive on his wonderful train and offer you a cure in exchange for you accompanying him." The Alchemist turned to Milo. "He was under strict instructions not to leave without her, hence my confusion that she is here, and yet he is not."

"But my uncle wanted Tilly to . . ." Milo stopped. Horatio had wanted Tilly to get the poison compendium for the Botanist, not to bring her here. He heard his uncle's voice in his head telling him that there was more than one story going on. He was abruptly incredibly aware of the fact that Horatio had signed a contract that said there was no family who would be in line to inherit the Quip. But the Alchemist already seemed to know his name and who he was.

Tilly, meanwhile, was staring at the Alchemist.

"So, it was a trap?" she said, her face drained of color.

"That's a very crass way of describing it," the Alchemist said. "But yes, technically, you would be correct."

"And do you even have a cure?" Milo asked. The Alchemist was so hard to speak with and Milo kept losing track of what they were talking about. The Alchemist was leading them where he wanted, finding out what he needed to know before Milo had even realized what he was giving away. Their focus had to be the cure.

"Why of course," the Alchemist said, and gave another nod of his head at Tommaso. "If Matilda agrees to my proposed arrangement, I will ensure that the antidote is sent promptly to London for her grandfather. Do not worry—he is not in any danger. Yet. And look, I'll send Archibald Pages a beautiful bottle from my wine cellar as well, as an apology for the inconvenience. Ah, here . . ."

Tommaso returned holding a small carved wooden box that he laid on the table next to the Alchemist's plate.

"You see," the Alchemist said, opening the box. "The cure." He pulled out a tiny glass vial of dark-purple liquid. "The poison on the book is one of my own creations—it is far more complex than you could imagine, and the only means of negating its effects is a dose of this. It needs only the final ingredient to activate it, and I will ensure your grandad receives it, Matilda."

"What's the final ingredient?" Tilly asked straightaway.

"I would be disappointed if you did not ask," the Alchemist said smiling, "but of course I cannot tell you. I will say only that it is the element that all my experiments and potions are rooted in, the thing that gives them power, and crucially, the thing that gives them specificity. And that is all you need to know."

"So what do you want from Tilly in exchange?" Milo asked nervously.

"Patience," the Alchemist said. "Look, here is our food."

Milo sat still, trying to process what they'd learned—that apparently his uncle had betrayed Tilly, poisoning her grandad so he could promise a cure and deliver her to the Alchemist. If Horatio hadn't touched the book, would they have been on their way here or to the Botanist? How on earth had his uncle ended up in debt to this man? And yet there was the fact that when he knew he only had moments left, his uncle had chosen to send Milo and Tilly to get the poison box. Would Horatio have tried to save Tilly if he hadn't been poisoned? Milo had the horrible feeling that they'd made an awful mistake in coming here and played right into the Alchemist's plans. As he went over and over it in his mind, Tommaso and the woman brought out plates of food.

"*È capesante alla griglia, crema di zucca e finferli,*" he said proudly.

Milo and Tilly stared at him, nonplussed.

"Grilled scallops with pumpkin cream and chanterelles," the Alchemist translated, to more blank stares. He sighed and pointed at one element. "Shellfish." He pointed at the orange sauce. "Sauce made from squash." He pointed at the vegetables. "And mushrooms."

Milo did not want to eat, more as a point of principle than because he was worried about being poisoned anymore, but the food smelled incredible, and he was very, very hungry. Tilly shrugged at him from across the table and picked up her fork. Milo reminded himself that he had the keys to the Quip if they needed to get away quickly. And they'd be no good on empty stomach, Milo said to himself, very convincingly.

He tentatively took a forkful, and it tasted even better than it smelled.

"So, what do you want from me?" Tilly asked as she ate. "What was important enough that you felt it was okay to poison my grandad just to get me here?"

"Believe me, Matilda, it is important," the Alchemist said. "I can understand your fixation on your grandfather's health, you are only young, but trust me when I say he is in no danger so long as you do as I ask. I am in search of a book."

"Isn't that what you paid my uncle for?" Milo interjected. "To provide you with books? I've seen the contract, you know. You can't pretend."

"Now, now," the Alchemist interrupted. "All in good time.

Let us start with Matilda before we move on to dear Horatio."

Milo contemplated pushing it, but the Alchemist had all the power, and they needed to know what he wanted from Tilly in exchange for the antidote. He kept eating and listening, albeit begrudgingly.

"There is a book," the Alchemist went on, "known as *The Book of Books*. It is extraordinarily old, and I am very keen to read it. I need your help, Matilda, to retrieve it."

"I've never even heard of it," Tilly said. "I don't know where it is."

"I know," the Alchemist said. "But I believe *I* do. I have not brought you here to track it down but to bring it back to me."

"Why don't you go and get it yourself?" Milo asked. "If you know where it is."

"Because it is a magical book," the Alchemist replied. "With very particular properties. And it is protected in various ways, including limits on who can find and open it."

Tilly let out a resigned sigh, to Milo's surprise.

"I'm guessing, given how much you clearly know about my family, that this is to do with me being half-fictional," she said.

"Quite," the Alchemist said. "I am . . . entertained to see that you appear to find power such as yours so much of an inconvenience." He was not smiling. "I have reason to believe that you, and perhaps only you, will be able to retrieve the book. You will see why I had to go to such extreme measures."

"No, I *don't* see why you had to, actually," Tilly said, and

Milo was in awe of how cross she was being. "It's just a book! It's not worth risking someone's life for!"

"It is not *just* a book, I can assure you," the Alchemist said, his charm never cracking. "Ah, let us pause while Tommaso and Maria clear our plates." The two of them silently whisked away the plates, which were replaced by more food.

"*Triglie scottate, vongole, carciofi e purée di sedano rapa*," the Alchemist said. "Or red mullet with clams, artichokes, and celeriac purée. Or, indeed, fish with more fish, and you surely must know what an artichoke is." He looked somewhat pained to be dining with such uncultured palates.

"Now," he continued. "Given that I hope we are about to enter into a most profitable business agreement, Matilda, I am happy to share with you a little more information. It is not a book. It is *the* book. *The Book of Books*. It holds within it the secrets of bookwandering and book magic itself. It holds the answers to why some readers can travel within books and some can't. It will tell us where we came from. Imagine what we could do with that knowledge! Imagine what we could achieve!"

"I'm sorry if this is a stupid question," Milo said, feeling several steps behind Tilly and the Alchemist. "I do understand that it would be really interesting to know why bookwandering exists, but what exactly would you want to do with that information? Why is it such a big deal? It's just information."

"I am surprised, given who your uncle is, that you do not understand the value of information better," the Alchemist said. "Especially information that others do not have access to. I am part of a very select group of bookwanderers who collect such knowledge, for the betterment of all. We are dedicated to understanding the intricacies of the imagination and its power. Who wouldn't want to learn all they could about these things? The possibilities are . . . well, they are infinite. They are eternal."

"And where exactly is this book?" Tilly said.

"It is in the possession of a rival book collector," the Alchemist said, his eyes turning cold with barely suppressed anger. "She goes by the name of the Botanist."

35

I See You Read the Small Print

Milo couldn't help but let out a small gasp, which he immediately tried to turn into an unconvincing yawn.

"Sadly, I am not surprised that you know my rival's name, Milo," the Alchemist said. "Since I know that your uncle was working for her, despite my explicitly forbidding this under the terms of our agreement."

"Your agreement," Milo said quietly. "He promised you the Quip."

"Now, Milo, before you judge me too harshly, one thing you need to understand is that until very recently, I did not even know that you existed. Your uncle has been keeping a great deal of information from both of us and weaving quite the elaborate web of lies. I assure you that when I drew up that contract, I sincerely had no idea he had any family who might inherit that beautiful train after he retired. Clearly, you have seen the contract; in which case, you will have also seen that I saved his life, and he promised me the Quip in return. There is no sinister scheme at play here. I believed I was simply guaranteeing ownership of something I admired a great deal after Horatio's tenure as the driver. Now it seems that agreement is in jeopardy—for part of the Quip's magic is that it passes automatically along a family line, and it transpires that Horatio does have an heir. You. This directly contradicts the guarantee he made in the contract. I do not approve of breaking contracts—I have killed people for less."

The Alchemist said this last part with a smile, as though it were proof he was a good person, as opposed to someone with an alarmingly casual approach to other people's lives.

Milo blinked at him.

"Regardless," the man continued, "it was a perfectly simple and clear arrangement, so I find myself surprised and confused as to why Horatio would break it by hiding your existence from me, especially after I saved him from that horrible accident that killed your parents—what an absolute tragedy."

"What?" Milo breathed, his fork clattering to his plate.

"How sad," the Alchemist said, looking at Milo with pity written across his face. "Evidently, your uncle has been keeping even more from you than I first imagined. I am so sorry to be the one who has to tell you this, Milo. Your parents died in a horrible and entirely preventable accident in which your uncle was also involved. Why, it would seem that you know very little about the Quip and what was happening onboard before Horatio took over."

"I know some things," Milo said defensively, thinking of the poster he'd found in the scrapbook. "I know my grandmother was called Evalina and that she used to be the driver. And that she ran it as some kind of . . . fairground thing."

"I am surprised Horatio told you even that much, given that Lina ended up in such disgrace," the Alchemist said. "It was her plan that caused the accident after all. She sent everyone off to *The Wizard of Oz* to try the Wizard's hot air balloon because she had an idea to use it as one of her carnival rides—such a classless use of bookwandering, if you ask me."

"We didn't," Milo heard Tilly mutter mutinously under her breath.

"Regardless, she dispatched you all there, with no thought for your safety and—"

"Wait," said Milo. "*I* was there too?"

"Oh yes. Did I not mention that? I am constantly surprised by how little your uncle has told you. Well, you are well-read children—I am sure you know that the Wizard is a fraud, and his balloon is barely airworthy. It was a lucky coincidence that I was passing and could help; tragically, it was too late for your parents, but I was able to help Horatio, at least."

"Once he'd promised you the Quip," Milo said.

"Oh, it was not so macabre," the Alchemist said. "Do you think I would leave a man to die if I could help? Of course not.

Yes, we were in heightened circumstances, but the terms of our contract were negotiated between two businessmen who knew what they were doing."

"But what about Milo?" Tilly asked. "I thought you didn't even know he existed until recently—but you just said *he* was in the balloon too."

"I assure you I have been learning much of this only very shortly before you . . . He kept you hidden from me when I found him at the crash," the Alchemist explained. "I do not know why; he clearly was already trying to pull the wool over my eyes. Or perhaps his infant nephew just slipped his mind in all the chaos. He certainly didn't see fit to mention it when we were negotiating our agreement. But, as we have discussed, Horatio has been grossly underestimating my access to information, and it was brought to my attention not long ago that you existed and lived on the train with your uncle. But anyway you are happy for me to take care of the Sesquipedalian for you, aren't you, Milo? If you were to sign something to that effect, I believe the magic of the Quip's succession might be broken."

"What?" Milo said in shock. "No, of course not! It isn't yours."

"I'm afraid your uncle's contract says otherwise," the Alchemist said, holding his hands out as though he regretted the turn of events. "So we reach an impasse."

"It says if he dies or retires, nothing about being poisoned," Milo pointed out.

"I see you read the small print," the Alchemist said. "How thorough. You are correct that we did not allow for this specific circumstance."

"So . . . you didn't mean for Horatio to be poisoned?" Tilly said.

"No, that was not part of the plan," the Alchemist admitted. "How curious to hear that is what has befallen him. Poetic justice, one might even say. Indeed, Horatio's attempts at . . . whatever he was trying to achieve and so clearly failed at have . . . changed the plan. I would say derailed, but as it happens we are all where we are supposed to be, despite the change of route. Horatio was at no point supposed to take the book back from your grandfather—he had no reason for doing it that I know of—and he knew it was poisoned, so he only has himself to blame for taking it and touching it. I would like to ask him a few questions about why he chose to retrieve the book." He paused and looked carefully at Milo and Tilly. "But perhaps it has all worked out for the best. The important thing for us all to focus on is that everyone has ended up in the right place."

"You mean that everyone has ended up in the right place for you," Tilly said.

"Yes, that is absolutely what I mean," the Alchemist said. "I have a much broader perspective than you could know, and the pieces are aligned."

"We are not *pieces*," Tilly said. "We are people."

"It is quite possible to be both," the Alchemist said. "We are all living our own lives, believing that we are charting our own course, but there is so much more going on, all the time. We are tiny dots in the universe, and I do not mean it as an insult to say we are pieces in a puzzle; what greater honor is there than to be a piece of a bigger story, a story that means something when you are gone? You are being offered the chance to be part of history!"

Despite everything the Alchemist had revealed, Milo was unsettled to find that he was struggling to concentrate on any of it as he was so sleepy. He kept trying to force his brain back onto what the Alchemist had said about his parents, but it was like wading through mud. It was very late, he thought, and they had eaten a lot of food. He saw Tilly try unsuccessfully to stifle a yawn.

"Now, look how tired you both are," the Alchemist said, smiling. "I think all of this can wait until the morning, don't you? Maria, would you show them to their rooms?"

Milo wanted to object, but he couldn't keep his eyes open; it was all he could do not to put his head down on the dining table and fall asleep then and there.

He could barely follow Maria up the stairs, and Tilly was in a similar state; clearly the last few hours were catching up with them. Maria pointed out a door to him, and then led Tilly to another farther down the corridor. The room was large and luxurious with thick cream carpet and heavy ruby velvet curtains drawn across the window. There was a huge four poster bed in the center of the room made up with fresh white sheets. A new pair of silky pajamas had been laid on top of the bed, but Milo was too tired to even consider getting changed. He managed to kick his boots off and let his satchel drop by the side of the bed before flopping down onto the soft pillows and falling asleep immediately.

36

A Fairly Casual Approach to Murder

"**N**o!" Milo protested, when someone shook him awake what felt like mere minutes later. "I want to sleep; please let me sleep."

"You have to wake up," a voice said urgently. "You've already been asleep for a couple of hours, and I need to speak to you."

"Tilly, no, we can sleep a bit more—it's still nighttime," Milo said, not opening his eyes. "Just five more minutes, please."

"It's nearly sunrise," the voice came again. "And I'm not Tilly."

"What?" Milo said, confusion filtering through his exhausted mind. He managed to rouse himself, a shot of adrenaline coursing through him as soon as he saw that it was a stranger shaking him awake. He peeled his eyes open fully and saw that it was the girl from earlier, the Alchemist's daughter.

"It's you," Milo said.

"It is indeed me," the girl said. "But, if you call me 'you,' it'll get confusing quickly, so probably best to stick with Alessia."

"What are you doing in my bedroom?" Milo said groggily.

"I need to speak to you and Tilly, and it's *pretttty* important, if you class being alive as important."

"What?" Milo said again, still struggling to concentrate properly. It felt like he had lead in his brains. "I'm sorry—I can't wake up. It's been an intense few hours. Are you sure I can't just have a tiny bit more sleep . . . ?" He tried to lie down again, but Alessia pinched him sharply on his hand. "Ow!" Milo said. "That was rude!"

"I am trying to help you!" Alessia insisted. "And you can't wake up because my father has put magnolia bark in your dinner, and maybe even a drop of belladonna, depending on how long he wanted you to be out of it. Probably some lavender on your pillows for good measure, or one of his own personal concoctions."

"He's drugged us?" Milo said in horror.

"Yep," Alessia said. "It's kind of his thing. That and power. And wanting to have control of everything. And a fairly casual approach to murder. He has a few things, none of them good. Now, come on! Get up or I'll keep pinching you until you do."

Milo tried to force himself to sit up and stay awake; it was a horrible feeling, his body and brain telling him that all he wanted to do was sleep. "Maybe some fresh air might help?" he said, pushing back the duvet.

"Ha," Alessia said, and moved over to the window. She

pushed back the curtains to reveal thin but sturdy bars across the window, preventing them from opening. The light was gray and weak still.

"What time is it?" Milo said, reaching for his boots and pulling them on.

"About six a.m.," Alessia said. "So, you've had a few hours of sleep, but this is the only time we can leave. My father only rests for a couple of hours in the very early morning—he barely needs to sleep anymore."

"Did you say *we* can leave?" Milo said.

"Yes, I'm coming too," Alessia said, offering no further explanation, and Milo noticed for the first time that she was wearing a jacket and a large backpack.

He was relieved to see that his own satchel was still by his bed, but when he picked it up it felt way too light, and more worryingly there was no jangle of keys.

"Oh no," he said, dropping to his knees and tipping out the contents on the carpet.

All that fell out was his notebook, his pen, and the business card with the Alchemist's symbol on it.

The copy of *The Wizard of Oz* was gone—and so were the keys to the Quip.

37

Bad Timing

A wave of panic washed over Milo as he clutched at his neck to check if the whistle was still there. His fingers closed over the chain, and he fell back against the bed in relief. Thankfully, the Alchemist must have either not realized that the whistle existed or not realized where Milo was hiding it.

"He's stolen something?" Alessia asked with a frown. "That's another one of his things. Taking other people's stuff."

"Yes," Milo said, feeling weak with worry and weariness. "The keys. I still have the whistle though, and I don't think anyone could drive the Quip without it, but we can't get back aboard without the keys. Maybe we could break a window," he suggested weakly. "But these keys open everything in the Quip as well: Horatio's files, the conservation carriage where all the rare books are kept, the post box. I suppose some of that you could smash open . . ."

"It's okay—I know where they'll be," Alessia said calmly. She had an expression on her face as though she were trying to work out a particularly complicated math puzzle in her head. "I hadn't planned on having to go via his study, but we still have time if we can get Tilly awake quickly. Do you have everything else?"

Milo nodded and then paused, grabbed the fancy silk pajamas that had fallen to the floor, and shoved them in his satchel. Alessia suppressed a laugh and went to open the door slowly, before signaling for Milo to follow her. The longer he was awake, the more the effect of whatever plants and poisons the Alchemist had used lost their grip on him. The two of them slipped out of the bedroom and along the corridor to the room where Tilly was sleeping. She was snoring, and Milo felt a bit embarrassed as he gently shook her awake.

"He's stolen the keys to the Quip," Milo whispered urgently. "Alessia is going to help us get them back, and then we have to go."

"Huh?" Tilly said groggily. "No, I don't know you."

"Tilly, it's Milo! You need to wake up! We have to go!"

"But . . . but . . . what about my grandad?" Tilly said, rubbing her eyes as she came to. "We can't go before we have the cure."

"Don't worry about that—it's under control," Alessia said. "Also, if you stay here, you should know that my father is going to kill Milo."

"What?!" Milo squeaked, forgetting to keep quiet as Alessia slapped her hand over his mouth.

"Sorry, bad timing," she said. "But I thought it might be

helpful to know the stakes. I am sure he has asked you very nicely to go and get that book he's obsessed with, but he has no intention of sending the cure to your grandad until you are back with the book—if he sends it at all. I can help you cure your grandad; I swear. I've already stolen what we need." She took her hand away from Milo's mouth.

"Why does he want to kill me?!" Milo said immediately, torn between utter terror and feeling that it was completely farcical that anyone would be trying to kill him. He wasn't sure if he wanted to cry or laugh hysterically in response.

"Because he wants your train, of course," Alessia said. "He thought it was his because he didn't even know you existed until a few months ago! Your uncle thought he was just delivering Tilly, but my father wanted both of you. It's useless trying to outwit him; you just have to run and hide. Now, *please*, if we don't go immediately, we don't stand a chance. We can talk more when we're safe."

Milo looked at Tilly, who shrugged—what choice did they have? It wasn't hard to believe that the Alchemist was even worse than he seemed. Quite dramatically worse, Milo thought to himself. Tilly had clearly also just fallen into bed without getting changed, and she hadn't even managed to get her boots off, so she sleepily tumbled out of bed, hair all over the place. She stretched, gave her head a shake, and gave them a determined, if slightly bleary-eyed, nod.

"Let's go," she said.

"We have to be incredibly quiet," Alessia said. "My father is sleeping and so is Maria, but Tommaso may well be up early to get everything ready for my father when he wakes. No talking, and follow me."

The three of them crept back down the stairs, the carpet absorbing their footsteps until they reached the wooden-floored hallway. Milo tried to walk delicately on tiptoe, but every creak and tap seemed to echo horribly loudly in the silence. Alessia led them past the room with the fire and back, deeper into the house. At the end of the corridor, a spiral staircase wound tightly upward, and Alessia started to climb the metal steps, silently and gracefully, wincing at every clang that Milo and Tilly made behind her. At the top of the staircase was a small landing and a door. Alessia pulled out a set of keys from her pocket and grinned over her shoulder at Milo and Tilly.

"I like to think I haven't inherited too many of my father's qualities," she whispered. "But I may have picked up one or two habits along the way."

She gently slid a brass key into the lock, and the door swung open to reveal a long room with a sloped ceiling. It was large and full of stuff: a huge wooden desk, a blackboard covered in symbols and equations, a golden telescope pointing out of a window, and what looked like a small science lab at one end. There were glistening metal tables, all sorts of glass beakers and containers, jars and bottles full of goodness knows what, and piles and piles of books everywhere. But the most remarkable thing about the

room was that the walls were covered by a map of the world, with thousands and thousands of sparkling pinpricks of light spread across it. Most of the lights were a warm white color, some were blue, and even fewer were emerald green.

"It looks just like the map room at the Underlibrary," Tilly breathed.

"What's that?" Milo and Alessia asked at the same time.

"There's this room at the British Underlibrary in London—I think they all have one—where the walls are covered in a map like this, with lights like these. Those lights represent all the bookshops and libraries in the world," Tilly explained. "Are these lights the same thing?"

"Sort of," Alessia said as she closed the door quietly and locked it again. "But my father's map tracks copies of his favorite book, *The Wizard of Oz*. I don't know how he does it, but every one of these dots is a copy of the book. It can't be all of them in existence—I don't think—but it is a lot of them. He studies imagination, *book magic*—did he tell you? He can track it better than anyone else. So, the blue lights are the ones being read at the moment, by anyone, and the green ones are where someone is bookwandering inside. It's how he knew about the accident, Milo."

"Am I the last person to hear about it?" Milo said, feeling almost angry.

"I'm not supposed to know, I'm sorry," Alessia said. "But so far in my life my main purpose has been to spy on my father and learn as much as I can about what he knows. He refuses to teach me anything useful about it, so I eavesdrop and steal, and I have copies of his keys and I sneak in here and I read, and I try and work it out. I'm sorry about your parents."

"Thank you," Milo said quietly, but then looked up. "Does that mean you know more about the agreement he made with my uncle?"

Alessia looked uncomfortable.

"A little bit," she admitted. "Now *please* let's find your keys and talk about it when we're safely out of here? I promise I'll answer all your questions, as much as I can, but we can't be caught here."

Milo nodded his agreement.

"So, are we up in the roof?" Tilly asked, staring upward at the gabled slopes of the glinting map.

"Yes," Alessia replied. "This room spans the whole of the

house, right at the top. Makes sneaking in and out a little challenging, but I imagine that's the point. Now, let's find your keys and get out of here."

"How do you know they're in here?" Tilly asked.

"Because this is where he keeps anything important," Alessia said. "He doesn't trust a single other person when it comes to this room. Not Tommaso or Maria or me—no one is allowed in here. So, if there's something valuable to him, it will be here. He only took the keys recently, so hopefully they are somewhere obvious. Milo, you check his desk. Tilly, take the shelves at the back, and I'll try and cover everywhere else."

The three of them split up. Milo headed to the huge desk, where he immediately spotted a pile of the thick business cards with their circular symbol. There were heaps of papers covered in tiny writing Milo couldn't read, presumably in Italian, and symbols that meant nothing at all to him. A few books lay open, some in English, and Milo could see a couple of the words the Alchemist had talked about downstairs: "aether" and "quintessence."

And there, just sitting on the top, was the wooden box the Alchemist had shown them over dinner: the one with the single dose of the cure in it. Milo opened it to check, and the tiny vial of purple liquid was still nestled inside.

Without thinking, Milo picked it up and slid the whole box into his satchel before turning his attention to the desk drawers. They were all unlocked apart from one that wouldn't budge. Milo started quickly moving through the others, and then there, in a shallow drawer, on top of a pile of letters wrapped in a ribbon, were the keys.

"I've got them!" he called as loudly as he dared, and Alessia came over immediately.

"Amazing," she whispered. "Let's go."

But as Alessia gestured for Tilly to come and join them, there was the unmistakable clang of footsteps running quickly up the spiral staircase.

All of Alessia's confidence evaporated instantly.

"He knows we're here," she said, her eyes wide and panicked.

"Is there another door?" Milo said as they heard a shout.

"I know the three of you are in there," came a bellow. "And you will regret the hour that you chose to cross me."

"He's nearly here," Alessia said, frozen in terror. "What do we do?"

"I don't know!" Tilly shouted. "I thought you had a plan!"

"My plan involved getting in and out of here before he had even woken up!" Alessia said.

Milo tried to focus. There were no other doors, as Alessia said, so he ran to one of the full-length windows, each with a small balcony outside. He peered through the glass and could see that the back of the house went straight down into a narrow canal, the pathway on the other side.

"We'll have to jump," he shouted back to the girls. "Can you swim?"

"What?!" Tilly said, horrified. "We can't jump! We'll break our necks!"

"I don't think we have another choice," Milo said, the need to get away from a man who already wanted him dead *before* he'd broken into his office overwhelming all other concerns.

Alessia, pale-faced and silent, nodded. She tried the ornate golden handle on the window, but it was locked as well, and before Milo realized what she was doing she pulled her hand back into her sleeve and punched the glass. A cascade of window shards rained down on them, and Milo flung his arms over his face to protect his eyes.

"Good *grief*," Tilly said, staring at Alessia in amazement. The three of them climbed through the ragged edges of the shattered window and onto the tiny balcony. They were three floors up, the air was icy, and the water was opaque underneath them. They heard the door start to rattle and a key being put in the lock.

"It's now or never," Milo said, climbing onto the edge of the balcony railing and swinging his legs over.

"Okay," Tilly said as she and Alessia joined him.

"*Uno, due* . . ." Alessia started, but then the door smashed open and they caught a glimpse of the Alchemist as he exploded into the room, and before she got to *tre* the three of them leaped into the canal below.

38

It's Not Easy When
Your Father Is an Evil Supergenius

The cold water hit Milo like a solid thing as he crashed into it, taking his breath away for a few awful seconds. Thankfully, the water was deep enough that they didn't hit the bottom, and Milo surfaced quickly, staring upward to see the Alchemist's irate face above them. There was an awful second when Milo thought that he was going to jump after them, but instead he *whirled* round and disappeared.

Then the second horrible realization washed over him as he thought of the cure inside his satchel, and he flung himself toward the far edge of the canal where the path was and chucked the bag up onto the ground, hoping not too much damage had been done. He hauled himself up and out onto the path, glancing around to see Tilly and Alessia bobbing nearby.

"We have to get out and onto the Quip!" Tilly yelled,

swimming toward him. "He'll be right behind us."

Milo helped Tilly and Alessia up, and they looked around, desperately trying to get their bearings.

"Where do we go?" Milo said, pulling the sopping wet scrap of paper that had been their map out of his bag.

"I know," Alessia said. "I was watching you when you arrived. This way, quickly."

Milo and Tilly followed Alessia, their wet clothes heavy and squelching. She darted through narrow alleyways and across a small bridge until they turned a corner that Milo recognized. One more corner and then there she was—and Milo had never been more delighted to see a train floating above a canal.

"She's still there," he breathed in relief, fumbling for the keys. They raced the last few feet to the Quip, and Milo unlocked the office carriage with wet, shaking fingers. The three of them jumped in and Tilly slammed the door behind them, but there was no time to stop, not until they had left Venice. Milo pulled the whistle out from beneath his sopping jumper and tried to focus. The whistle tasted deeply unpleasant from the canal water, but he ignored it and instead focused on where he wanted to go, closed his eyes, and blew.

The Quip stretched into life around them and started to rumble.

"We'll need to top her up with magic very quickly," Milo said. "But she should have enough to get us out of here."

The three of them went to the window, and the last thing they saw was the Alchemist skidding round the corner to watch them disappear as Venice began to come to life in the hazy pastel light of the sunrise.

Once they were safely out of Venice, the three of them sank to the floor in a very damp, relieved heap.

"Oh my goodness me," Tilly said, squeezing canal water from her hair. "That was far too close."

Alessia looked as though she might be about to throw up.

"Well, all things considered, that could have gone worse," Milo said. Tilly raised an eyebrow at him.

"We're all alive for one thing, if very wet, Alessia escaped, and we know more than when we arrived, plus . . ." He pulled the box out of his satchel. "I stole this."

"Milo! You're amazing!" Tilly said. "But . . . it's only one dose."

"It's okay. I've already decided it's for your grandad," Milo said. Tilly started to argue, but he shook his head. "I know Alessia said she had more, but we can't risk it. I've thought about it and it's what I want. He's been asleep for longer, and he doesn't have anything to do with this—the Alchemist was just using him to get to you. I want Horatio to wake up eventually, but we need to make sure your grandad is awake before Horatio is in charge again. Plus, he's a part of this in a way that your grandad isn't—so this is what's right and what's fair. I've made up my mind."

"Oh Milo," Tilly said. "Thank you." And she rushed across the carriage and flung her arms round him. It was very damp, and they both smelled pretty bad, but it was still the nicest hug Milo had ever had.

"You've forgotten one thing," Alessia said quietly. "Didn't my father tell you? It needs a last ingredient to activate it."

Milo had forgotten about that. "But you know what that ingredient is, right?" Milo said.

"Sort of," Alessia said.

"I thought you said you knew all about it!"

"I didn't!" Alessia protested. "I just said I had what we needed—I have the recipe! And the recipe says what we need, so don't get angry with me. I'm trying to help."

"So you *do* know what the ingredient is?"

"Yes and no."

"What?!" said Milo.

"Let me explain!" said Alessia, her voice breaking. "Please!"

"Sorry," Milo said. "We just want to help Archie, and we need answers from Horatio."

"I know," Alessia said. "I'm sorry—it's just . . . I've barely been out of that house at all, and it was horrible there. I'm readjusting. It's not easy when your father is an evil supergenius, you know."

"I bet," Tilly said. "So . . . about that last ingredient?"

"I know what it *is*, but I don't know what it *means*," Alessia said. "The poison is made for each person individually; my father talks about specificity all the time, and all his magic is curated— and so the poison has this personalized ingredient that you also need for the cure."

"But what is it?" Milo and Tilly said at the same time.

"It says on the recipe that in order to make the poison—or the cure—work, it has to contain what it calls 'the record of that reader.'" Alessia curled her fingers into air quotes as she recited the ingredient. "And I'm so sorry, but I have no idea what that means."

Milo and Tilly exchanged a triumphant glance.

"That's okay," Milo said with a smile. "We do."

TILLY

39

A Deal with the Devil

Half an hour later the three of them were clean and dry after using the showers in the guest quarters. Tilly had even managed to find a hair dryer in the beautifully decorated room Milo showed her to. They'd tried their best to rinse out their clothes and had hung them up in the hot engine room as they'd rolled more *book magic* orbs into the fire. They were now gathered in the dining carriage wearing the fluffy dressing gowns that Horatio provided for his most prestigious or wealthy clients.

Milo had managed to pull together breakfast, and they munched on toast and peanut butter with glasses of orange juice to drink, followed by mugs of hot tea and a packet of biscuits.

"I think it's time you told us everything you know," Tilly said to Alessia once they were fed.

"I can tell you as much as I do know," Alessia said. "But I'm afraid there are a lot of gaps. As you have seen, my father is incredibly secretive and hasn't shared anything with me on purpose. It's only from sneaking around and listening in that I know anything at all. And I was listening when you were talking to him first too, so I know he's told you about *The Book of Books*. He's obsessed with it. He thinks it holds the answers to everything. I think it's likely that he knows more about bookwandering than anyone else who's alive, but he still can't work out where it came from, and why some people can do it and some people can't. And he is convinced that only you will be able to find this book that will tell him, Tilly, because you are half-fictional. Part of the legend around it is that only one reader can find it and read it."

"But what I don't understand," Tilly said, "is why he needs to know. You say the book holds the answers, but what's the question? He was talking about all that stuff to do with alchemy and the imagination—what's he actually trying to do?"

"Alchemists used to be focused on trying to make the philosopher's stone," Alessia explained. "It would have let them live forever. My father *is* an alchemist but not one that studies gold and salt and sulfur. He studies imagination."

"He told us that," Milo pointed out.

"Right, but I bet he didn't tell you that he's worked out a way to distill book magic down and create an elixir that not only extends his life but also lets him bookwander without the need for a book."

"But . . ." said Tilly. "But that means he could go . . . basically anywhere?"

"Yes. He can travel within almost any book at will—the

elixir and his map of *The Wizard of Oz* are why he could find your uncle and offer him a deal just after the accident, Milo. They're why he could get inside a book that your family owned. He's free of the normal rules of bookwandering. He doesn't need a book or a train to travel, he can simply go."

"But, if he can do that, then what does he need this *Book of Books* for?" Tilly asked.

"Because he won't stop until he has complete mastery; that's just the start of things for him. He has all sorts of potions and elixirs, but at the moment a lot of what he can do is limited to *The Wizard of Oz*. He can't see into all books, but his potions are broadening his power every day. He wants to know everything there is to know about bookwandering and the magic of imagination so he can control it. He hoards information—he has a secret storeroom in the Emerald City where he keeps it all."

Milo and Tilly glanced at each other but didn't mention that they'd been to that very place only hours ago.

"He wants to have power over the world's knowledge," continued Alessia. "So he can run it without anyone even knowing it's him. The possibilities would be limitless if he held all of the world's knowledge and imagination in his hands. My father . . . He's older than he looks."

"He said that too," Milo said warily. "What exactly does that mean? How old is he?"

"I don't know precisely," Alessia answered. "But I know

that he was alive when alchemists were working on the philosopher's stone in Venice—back in the sixteenth century."

"I'm sorry, what?" Tilly said in disbelief. "But that was over five hundred years ago."

"Yes," Alessia said. "Like I said, older than he looks. And it's also why he doesn't care about anyone or anything else, I think. He's had far too long to get good at being evil and stop caring about people."

"But how old are you?" Milo asked in confusion.

"Oh, I'm just normal," Alessia said merrily. "I'm thirteen. My father is, despite everything, a romantic, and has fallen in love with many women over the centuries. But my mother did not want a baby, or that's what he told me. Unfortunately, neither did my father, but when she left me on his doorstep he didn't really have a choice. Maria looks after me mostly."

"Why do adventures always happen to people with complicated families?" Milo wondered out loud.

"I guess that people with normal families are too busy doing normal things," Tilly said. "No time for adventures. But, speaking of families, mine will be worrying as soon as they're awake. Have we got any way of knowing what time it is at home?"

"I woke you up just before six," Alessia said. "It's, what, maybe an hour later? So, seven in Venice, and I think England is an hour behind."

"So six o'clock or thereabouts then," Tilly said. "I think I've got an hour or so before anyone notices I've gone. Hopefully, we can get Grandad's Record—and Horatio's—quickly and get home. Do you think he would have ever sent the cure back, if I'd helped him?"

"Probably not," Alessia said. "He definitely wouldn't have sent it until he had the book, and he probably would still hold it over you then, to get you to do something else for him. It's what he does; he makes deals with people, but he creates the circumstances so you have to do it, and then he changes the details forever. You can never win. It's like his deal with Milo's uncle, and why he can't have Milo alive."

"Oh yeah, that," Milo said quietly. "Do you think he caused the accident that killed my parents?"

"I don't know," Alessia said. "I just know that he knew about it very quickly and that he had wanted your train—you call this the Quip, right?—well, that he'd wanted the Quip ever since he knew she existed and that, until very recently, he hadn't known you were around and would inherit it."

"But why is it such a big deal?" Milo asked. "If he's convinced Horatio to sign this contract—even if it was in suspicious circumstances—isn't that it? What can I do? I'm powerless."

"No," Alessia said. "He can't exactly take it to a regular lawyer to uphold, and neither my father nor your uncle respect the authority of the Underlibraries. That contract means nothing if you are alive. He doesn't really believe that either you or Horatio have the power to sign her over to him. She is passed from driver to driver and is yours—and look, you can clearly drive her. The Quip won't answer to my father until you are dead; it's in your blood."

"So why would Horatio promise it to him if he knew that?"

"It sounds like my father held Horatio's life in his hands, and your uncle did what he thought he needed to do to stay alive and to protect you. Even if it meant making a deal with the devil. I suppose he was trying to keep you safe until he could come up with a better plan."

"A better plan," Milo repeated slowly. "Horatio was working on something else! Something that he needed the poisons for—and something to do with the Botanist. Do you think he's been working against the Alchemist all along?" Milo's face looked so hopeful that his uncle might be a hero after all.

"Let's just remember he was willing to trade me to the Alchemist," Tilly said, not wanting to kill that hope but feeling like this was fairly relevant information.

"We don't know that he would have gone through with it," Milo said. "He maybe had this whole other plan! That's why he told us to go to the Botanist, not the Alchemist. Maybe this whole time he was hiding me with the Marters to protect me!"

"Maybe," Tilly said, but she was unconvinced. She'd seen the way Horatio baited and switched allegiances depending on what he wanted. She'd take her chances with Horatio over the Alchemist any day, but that didn't mean she trusted him, even if he was unconscious.

40

All Sorts of Uses for Book Magic

The time sped by as they chatted, and despite the enormity of the things facing them, Tilly started to feel like maybe, with the recipe from Alessia, they'd be okay. She felt sure that Artemis would know something useful too. Tilly was a bit nervous about Alessia's recipe; whether she could make it and whether it would work. But a real recipe was better than a promised cure from someone they couldn't trust at all. At least they had one dose of the cure for Grandad, or they would once they had his Record—and Artemis would certainly be able to help with that.

Soon, they felt the Quip start to slow, and the darkness faded into light as they arrived at the Archive. They changed back into their now-dry clothes, and Milo gathered up his satchel. Tilly was feeling buoyed up and determined as she flung open the train door, but then she saw what was waiting for them.

"It's even more run down than when I was here yesterday," Milo said in horror. "How can it have got so much worse so quickly?"

Milo had already warned Tilly that the Archive was in a bad way, but she hadn't imagined it could be this grim. The three of them stared at the cracked stones and rubble that made up what had been a beautiful station last time Tilly had been here. Yes, there had been some problems, but nothing compared to this. It was barely recognizable as a train platform anymore, she thought, as they picked their way over the mess toward the once elegant gates, which now lay on the ground, broken and dirty. The path leading to the Archive was now mainly dirt and debris, and the house was barely standing, with crumbled wreckage where sections had given up completely and collapsed.

"You're sure this is the right place?" Alessia said skeptically as the three of them climbed the broken steps to the front door.

"Yes," Tilly said, although she was dreading what they might find.

The front door wasn't closed properly, and so Milo stepped forward and pushed it open. It creaked ominously, and the three of them tentatively went in.

"Hello?" Tilly called. "Artemis? It's Tilly and Milo!"

"And Alessia," Milo added.

"You came back," a voice said, and from a doorway appeared Artemis. Tilly found it hard not to gasp in shock. Artemis's hair was completely loose, tangled, and knotty. Her skin had smears of what looked like soot on it, her clothes were ripped and tattered, and she was no longer wearing any shoes.

"Milo, Matilda," she said, as polite as ever, despite her appearance. "How lovely it is to see you again. And you've brought a new friend."

"This is Alessia della Porta," Tilly said. "She's been helping us with . . . well, a few things. I'm sorry to barge in on you, but we need your help."

"It's a pleasure to meet you, Alessia," Artemis said, but she was frowning slightly. "'Della Porta,' did you say? What an interesting name. Italian?" She paused and locked eyes with Alessia but then smiled and continued. "I can only apologize for the state of this place. We have seen better days. Why don't you tell me what is going on, and we'll see what I can do. Your uncle isn't with you, Milo?"

"No," Milo said. "That's part of the problem—quite a lot has happened since I saw you yesterday."

"Well, come in and make yourselves comfortable," Artemis said. "The Archive itself is the safest place these days."

The three of them exchanged surprised glances. Artemis was behaving as though they were standing in a luxurious hotel, not a crumbling ruin. Alessia in particular looked disturbed, but of course she hadn't seen the Archive when it was working and beautiful, Tilly reminded herself. She gave Alessia what she hoped was a reassuring nod, and the three of them followed Artemis down one of the dark corridors, toward the hall of Records.

The last time that Tilly had been in the actual Archive itself, where all the Records were stored, it had been a place of order and cleanliness. She could barely take in the state of it as they followed Artemis inside. Hardly any books were left on the shelves, and loose pages were blowing in the breeze wafting through cracks in the walls. Tilly gave Milo a worried look and saw Alessia stare around them in disquietude.

"This is the safest place to be," Artemis repeated. "It is the most stable room left and where I have been spending most of my time. I am afraid I cannot offer you much in the way of refreshment, but I hope I can help with whatever you have come here for. And Milo, might I hope you have returned Theodore's Record to me? I would feel more settled if it were returned; I should not have let your uncle take it, and I have been regretting it since I let it out of this place. I should not allow even the slightest piece of *book magic* to leave."

"I have," Milo said, pulling the white book out of his satchel. He gave it back to Artemis, who stroked its cover like it was a runaway cat returned safely. "But, the thing is," he started nervously, "we came here because we need to borrow some more. Or take a bit of them? We're not quite sure." He petered out and glanced at Tilly, who was having the same realization that she wasn't quite sure of the mechanics of adding a big book to a tiny vial of liquid. She looked around to ask Alessia, but she had wandered off to look at the Records.

"You are not permitted to look at those," Artemis said sharply.

"But you let Milo's uncle take one," Alessia pointed out. "And they are not being looked after—they are all ripped and destroyed."

"I am trying my best," Artemis said desperately to Tilly and to Milo as she reluctantly left Alessia to her own devices, picking over the mess of Records.

"Is this all because of the Archivists leaving?" Tilly said quietly, feeling horribly guilty. "I'm so sorry that I had something to do with that. If Will hadn't left maybe none of this would have happened—but we wouldn't have been able to save the British Underlibrary if it wasn't for Will in the end!"

"You do not need to apologize," Artemis said, putting a reassuring hand on Tilly's arm. "I encouraged Will to go as well—I was interested to see what . . . Well, I thought he would be a help to you, and none of us ever know what the ultimate consequences of our actions will be. I share any blame. We all do things we shouldn't at times," she added. "Speaking of which, Milo, you borrowed something else while you were here last."

Milo blushed, and Tilly saw his hand go to his satchel. He must have brought the scrapbook with him.

"I'm sorry I took it without asking," he said. "But . . . I'm not returning it. Why is it here? And where is my Record? I don't think I should have to give this back—it's my family photos and letters—they don't belong here."

"I am inclined to agree," Artemis said. "But it was kept here as part of an agreement with your uncle, and I would need to have your true Record back for you to keep the scrapbook you have taken."

"Horatio gave it to you?" Tilly said, not following.

"Yes," Artemis said gently. "He discovered us by following a map he found, and, when he realized what the Archive was storing, he brought that scrapbook the next time he visited—the time that you arrived, Tilly. That was part of what our meeting was about. He traded it for Milo's Record."

"But why?" Milo asked.

"I understand that Horatio was keen to be able to . . . well, keep an eye on you, know where you were bookwandering, who you were talking to," Artemis said slowly.

"But how did it work?" Tilly asked. "I thought that the Archive could only see where we bookwander because of the potency of the *book magic* here."

"Yes, that's right," Artemis said. "But according to Horatio the levels of *book magic* on the Quip were more than enough to keep the Record working properly, and it would seem he was right. I am sorry that you've had to find out that your uncle was spying on you."

"I'm not sure he was spying exactly!" Tilly said. "We just learned . . ." She paused and checked with Milo that he was happy for her to explain what they'd learned from the Alchemist. Milo nodded his agreement. "We just learned that Milo's uncle was keeping him hidden to try and keep him safe," Tilly explained. "He didn't want the Alchemist to know that Milo existed because the Alchemist wanted the Quip! But what I don't understand is—"

"The Alchemist?" Artemis repeated, her face pale.

"Do you know him?" Tilly asked in confusion. "Has he been here?"

"Who is Alessia?" Artemis said, her face suddenly steely. "Has he sent her?"

"What? No!" Milo said. "She's his daughter, and she escaped with us! Don't worry—you can trust her!"

"Where is she?" Artemis looked around in a frenzy, searching for Alessia.

Tilly looked at Milo, unnerved, as Alessia heard Artemis calling and came over, not looking especially ruffled or concerned.

"Are you okay?" she said.

"Did your father send you? Does your father know you're here?"

"Not specifically," Alessia said. "But he knows I've escaped.

Don't worry, though. I'm not on his side or anything. Why? What do you know of him? Are you hiding from him? Has he been here?"

"No . . . no . . . I have . . . heard of him," Artemis said, still looking distinctly rattled. "He is a very powerful man. I do not want to draw attention to myself."

"Don't worry. He doesn't know we came here," Tilly tried to reassure her. "Although we did want to ask you about him. Do you know what he's been doing? That he's worked out how to bookwander without books?"

"What?" Artemis said, wide-eyed and frantic.

"Yes," said Tilly. "He can just travel wherever he wants through Story without using a book!"

"He is an accomplished story alchemist," Alessia said. "He has discovered all sorts of uses for *book magic*: the secret to immortality and, as Tilly says, wandering without books."

"And you know what this secret is?" Artemis pressed.

"Yes," Alessia said. Tilly and Milo looked at her. "Well, sort of," she amended. "I have the recipe for his bookwandering elixir; I have almost all of his recipes. But I've never tried to make this one before."

"I see," Artemis said, calming down. "Well, I would be fascinated to see it. I'm sure that Milo and Tilly have told you that I have dedicated my life to studying the potential of *book magic* and imagination, as much as I can from this place anyway!" She gave a tight laugh.

"You cannot leave?" Alessia asked.

"No," Artemis said, and it was as though all the fight had suddenly drained out of her. She slumped against a bookcase and looked exhausted. "I cannot."

"That is why you would like the recipe?" Alessia said quietly. "So you can leave? I don't know that it would let you—what is it that's keeping you here?"

"I don't know," Artemis admitted. "Otherwise, I would have been able to research it more fully. I am not . . . I am not quite human, really, I fear, although I feel that I am, in many, many ways. I am not a bookwanderer in any traditional sense; I cannot live in your world."

"So where did you come from?" Milo asked.

"I think I was written into existence," Artemis said. "But I do not truly know. For a long time, there was a group of bookwanderers who would come here to work and read and also experiment with *book magic*, but I do not hear from them as much anymore. I have been left to my own devices and my own ruin. When this place finally crumbles, I believe I will go with it. There is not enough *book magic* being channeled into it. The Records are all that seem to work still as *book magic* seems to be funneled into them, but I do not know from where. I have failed in my one purpose: to protect this place."

Tilly felt horrible for her.

"Do you think it would work?" Tilly asked Alessia. "Would the elixir help Artemis leave? Could you save her?"

Alessia looked uncomfortable. "I really don't know," she said. "And I don't know if I have the skill to do it or that we have the equipment we need. It might not even work at all if she's not a bookwanderer, or a real person—no offense."

"None taken." Artemis smiled, a little tightly. "Now, I understand you're a little on the spot here, Alessia, but perhaps we could make an exchange. You said that you needed some Records, correct? I do not imagine this place will last at all once I am gone, and these Records may well cease to exist. If you are willing to help me, I would be happy for you to take the Records that you need."

"But what would happen to you?" Tilly asked. "Aren't you scared?"

"Oh yes," Artemis said. "But that shouldn't stop you from doing something right or important or necessary."

"It's your decision," Tilly said to Alessia. "But I think we should help." She turned to Artemis. "Would it be okay if we grabbed those Records first? Two in particular—but we'd like to take some others as well, in case we need them later for . . . well, something that could be really important."

Artemis nodded her agreement. "Milo, why don't you go and round up the Records you have come for? While the girls see if they have what they need. Oh, and Milo?" He turned round. "Your grandmother's Record will be under 'T' for Treiber, her maiden name. I imagine you'll want that one too."

"It might not work," Alessia said again, but this time she

was rummaging around in her backpack, and she pulled out a notebook closed with a cord.

"I understand," Artemis said gently. "But I would like to try if you are willing. I think it's finally time for me to go."

41

The Anonymous Reader

"**D**o you have everything you need for the elixir?" Artemis asked.

"I think I need to go and get a few things from the Quip," Alessia answered. "I'll ask Milo." She disappeared off to get the keys from Milo and headed out of the Archive, studying the notebook closely as she walked.

"Given what I know of her father, I am sure the recipe is sound," Artemis said to Tilly. "And it sounds like it works for him, at least, if he could travel into *The Wizard of Oz* after the hot air balloon accident."

"Did we tell you that?" Tilly said, confused. "About the accident?"

"Oh no," Artemis said, smiling. "I know from the Records, of course."

"Oh, of course," Tilly said, although she didn't quite understand. "How can you know what's in *all* of them, though?"

"I don't really," Artemis said. "But remember that I have a lot of time here, and there are not as many bookwanderers as there used to be. And once I've met a bookwanderer I'm sure you'll understand that I am more interested in following their story. Wouldn't you be?"

"I guess," Tilly said, reminding herself that although it seemed like snooping, it was Artemis's job to keep track of and look after the Records.

Tilly abruptly realized that this might be the last chance she had to ask Artemis questions and felt suddenly overwhelmed by all the things she wanted to know. She decided to start with the most pressing, but Artemis got there first.

"How is your issue with Story progressing?" she asked. "When you visited me last, it was trying to reclaim you in some way."

"It doesn't happen very often anymore," Tilly said. "But it hasn't stopped completely—I have to be wary. Do you think that what's happening here is the reason it's slowed down? Because the *book magic* is vanishing as the Archive falls down?"

"Perhaps," Artemis said. "Or perhaps . . . Well, maybe Story came up with a new plan to get what it wanted."

"That sounds worse," Tilly pointed out.

Artemis looked around, as if she was expecting to see someone listening to their conversation. "It's hard for me to be able to help you as I would like, Tilly," she said.

"I don't understand."

"There's a lot that's . . . evolving at the moment," she said slowly. "And things are not always as they seem." Tilly was unnerved, but Artemis would not say any more.

"Can I ask you something about the Alchemist?" Tilly asked, trying a different tack. "Can you tell me about him?"

"I can try and be of use," Artemis said, without making eye contact with Tilly. "I'm not sure how helpful I will be, though."

"Well, he wants me to go and get this book called *The Book of Books*, and I wondered if you knew anything about it."

"Oh," Artemis said, sounding relieved. "That's not really to do with the Alchemist at all, although it's no surprise to me that he wants it."

"So you do know about it?"

"Of course," Artemis said. "It is a mythical book, supposedly one of the oldest books still to exist, and it is said to hold in it all the secrets of bookwandering—how it began and how it works. It's believed that it tells how you can make someone a bookwanderer, or take it away from them, and also how you can channel the magic that causes it. But we don't really know. The book hasn't been seen for a very long time."

"The Alchemist seemed to think only I could find it." Tilly pushed.

"Well, that's because part of the myth is that there's only one bookwanderer in every generation who can. The legend calls them the Anonymous Reader."

"But, if they're anonymous, why does he think it's me?"

"It's more of a title," Artemis explained. "They're a reader who represents all readers and writers. The Archive hosted the famous and the great and the revered; the Anonymous Reader represents all of us."

"That can't be me," Tilly said, overwhelmed.

"It could be," Artemis said. "But it could be anyone. The Alchemist believes it's to do with grandness or special abilities—it's why he thinks your half-fictional nature signals that it's you. But I believe it's a title you earn, that you take on without realizing. I think any reader has the potential, but how you know is beyond me. I suppose you find out if you try to discover or open *The Book of Books*."

"So, he just thinks it's me because my dad is a character from a book?" Tilly said. "Everyone always thinks that makes me special."

"It does, Tilly," Artemis said. "But it's not the only thing—it's important to remember that. Yes, your unusual heritage means you have remarkable bookwandering abilities, but you are also special because you are brave and curious and kind. You're smart and loyal and take care of your friends and family. I don't think it will do you any good to pretend that your abilities don't make you interesting, but, the other things, they're what really matter."

"Thank you," Tilly said quietly.

"Think about what you managed to accomplish in the

spring," Artemis said. "When you set so many Source Editions free, you gave them back to readers. Much of the Alchemist's power over *The Wizard of Oz* is rooted in his ownership of the Source Edition, and what you did has stopped him, or anyone else, from being able to control so many other books in the same way."

"But anyone could have done that if they'd thought of it," Tilly said. "And I couldn't have done it without Oskar, or you, or Will, or Milo."

"But no one else did think of it," Artemis said. "The Anonymous Reader who can open *The Book of Books* is someone who knows stories in a true and deep sense; your heritage helps you to be able to do that, but it's about your actions as much as your family history. As I said, I can see why the Alchemist thinks that it's you, and it could be, but it would be because of your relationship to stories, not because of who your parents are."

"So, only this one reader, the Anonymous Reader, can find it?" Tilly asked.

"Yes, and only they can open it, so the myth goes," Artemis said. "Although you know as well as I do that a myth is a story built around a grain of truth, not a rule book."

"The Alchemist said that the Botanist had it," Tilly said. "Do you know her?"

"I know of her, of course," Artemis said. "She is known to many as the Botanist because of her fascination with plants and folklore, but she also has a name: Rosa Clearwood. She is a great collector of books and stories."

"But if she has it, then doesn't that mean she's the Anonymous Reader?" Tilly asked.

"Perhaps, or maybe she doesn't have it, she just knows where it is, or it could be that she's laid a false trail for the Alchemist to follow."

"Because they're rivals?" Tilly questioned. "He really seemed to hate her. But . . . but Horatio wanted us to go to her. Do you know why?"

"I know that Horatio Bolt always has more schemes and plans and ideas going on than seems possible," Artemis said with a rueful smile.

At that moment Milo returned from the shelves, with a huge stack of white Records piled in his arms that he could barely hold.

"I got Archie's, and all your family's, and Oskar's, and Horatio's, and my parents' and my grandma's, and yours and Alessia's, just in case," he said, dumping them down on the floor and panting a bit. "Obviously mine isn't here but I think we should take as many as possible. I looked for the Alchemist's when I got Alessia's, but there wasn't one with the name from the contract."

"He doesn't have a Record," Artemis said.

"What? Why not?" Tilly asked, but Artemis just shrugged awkwardly.

"It's never been here," was all she said.

"So how do you know so much about him?" Tilly asked.

"Now, look, here's Alessia," Artemis said, not answering the question. "Do you have everything you need?"

"Yep," Alessia said, her arms full of various odd items, including some of the wooden balls that powered the Quip. "Or at least everything you won't already have here. I just need ink."

"That I can provide," Artemis said, her cheeks burning as though she had a fever and her eyes glassy and bright. She went over to the desk by the door, pulled out a bottle of glossy black ink, and brought it over to Alessia.

"I might need some more *book magic*," Alessia said. "I think the charged orb will have more than enough, but I've not done this before and I'm not quite sure how much my father uses."

"Gather up some of these papers," Artemis instructed Tilly and Milo. "They are full of *book magic*."

"From the Records?" Tilly said unsurely.

"Yes," Artemis said. "This whole place is falling down, Tilly, so these Records will all be gone very soon. And they are suffused with *book magic*, as you know; they will burn and release each reader's imagination, just like when Horatio burns the orbs."

"Ahhhh," Tilly said, understanding at last how they could add the Records to the cure. She saw that Milo and Alessia had had the same realization, and all three of them turned to check that the pile of Records Milo had collected was still there.

Alessia was studying the notebook closely, her forehead

creased in concentration. She had set a glass jug on the floor alongside a pair of metal cooking tongs, a box of matches, some of the charged wooden orbs that powered the Quip, and . . .

"Is that honey?" Tilly asked, looking at the half-full jar on the floor.

"Yep," Alessia said, not looking up. "It's sugar we need. You can use regular sugar, and way back when they used to use fruit, but honey works too, and this was the first thing I could find in the Quip's pantry. Right, so we need imagination contained in paper or wood, we need sugar, we need ink, and we need to heat it in a glass container over fire."

"That's it?" Artemis said.

"It's alchemy," Alessia said. "It's all about turning base—or regular—things into pure ones; it's about turning temporary things into eternal ones. You don't need a lot of fancy things; you just need to know what to do with them."

Tilly and Artemis watched silently as Alessia followed the instructions she had copied down in her notebook. She put one of the orbs carefully into the glass jug and lit a match, holding it to the orb until it caught, the flames licking up around it making it spark and glitter. Alessia tipped a small amount of honey over it, and a sweet, smoky smell filled the air, exactly like the smell of . . .

"Toasted marshmallows!" Tilly said in delight. "That's why bookwandering smells like toasted marshmallows!"

Next, Alessia tipped in the ink that Artemis had provided, and when the ink and honey combined with the burning *book magic* the orb disintegrated in on itself, like a collapsing star, and the jug was full of an iridescent black liquid with flames dancing on top and colors shimmering across its surface like a peacock's feathers.

"Wow," Milo said. "It's beautiful."

"Isn't it?" Artemis said, moving closer to the fiery liquid. "How do we know when it's done?"

"When the flames go out," Alessia said, wiping her hair out of her face and keeping her eyes trained on the liquid. After only a few more minutes, the flames roared up, a prism of bright rainbow light reflecting around the room, and then, as quickly as they had intensified, they died down, leaving a black powder in the jar with just the suggestion of sparkle to it.

"Did it work?" Tilly asked quietly.

"There's only one way to find out," Alessia said, looking up at Artemis.

"Do I just . . . ingest it?" Artemis asked, looking scared for the first time. "And then what do I do?"

"I don't know about the second one—I'm sorry," Alessia said. "But my father mixes a small amount into water and drinks it; here, I brought this." She reached back into her bag and pulled out a water bottle and a teaspoon that she used to scoop up a small amount of powder, before tipping it into the bottle. As she shook it gently they could see the powder disperse and disappear, and then Alessia handed it to Artemis.

There was absolute silence in the room as Artemis took it with a slightly shaky hand.

"Wish me luck," she said before tipping the bottle back and drinking deeply.

The three children watched her as she swallowed and smiled at them again. And then there was a bone-shaking rumble as though thunder were rolling right outside the building and the floor began to shake.

42

See You in Your Imagination

"**W**hat's happening?" Milo said as he tried to stay upright.

"I don't know," Artemis said, and then stopped, a rasping gasp coming from her throat. "What did you do?" she said to Alessia, who looked as though she might burst into tears.

"I tried to follow the recipe!" Alessia said desperately. "I told you I hadn't done it before! I'm so sorry. Oh no, oh no."

Tilly went to take her hand, to keep them standing as the whole place rattled and shook, and to try and reassure her, even though she was also terrified.

"It's not your fault," she shouted above the din. "We all agreed to try this. Are you okay, Artemis? Can we do anything? Can you move? We need to get to the Quip!"

"Oh!" Artemis said, tearing her gaze from Alessia. "Oh!" And then she closed her eyes, and a look of enormous peace came over her face, just as a huge chunk of the ceiling crashed to the floor, obliterating a shelf of Records.

"What's happening to her?" Milo whispered as Artemis held her hands out to her side, dropping the water bottle on the floor and letting it roll away. Sparks of *book magic* started to fly from her skin, as the Archive rumbled and roiled underneath their feet. She wasn't responding to the children at all now.

"She looks like . . . she looks like Will when he dissolved," Tilly said. "I think she's becoming pure *book magic*."

"Is that okay?" Alessia whispered, and tears were quietly rolling down her cheeks.

"But where will she go?" Milo asked.

"I don't know," Tilly said quietly. "She was never a person, not like Will, but whatever is happening, it means she's free. It was never going to work the same way it did on a book-wanderer, on a human. All she wanted was to leave, and I think she finally can."

They watched for a moment as the edges of Artemis started to fray and spark further, but more huge chunks of stone were falling from above, crashing into the shelves and toppling them over so they became a *wave of deadly dominoes.*

"We need to go!" Milo yelled, and it jolted them into action. Alessia started gathering up the things she'd brought and shoving them into her backpack, and Milo and Tilly picked up the pile of Records. Tilly could barely carry them they were so bulky and heavy, but they didn't have time to have a conversation about whether they could leave some of them behind. Many of them belonged to Milo's family, and it wasn't her decision whether to abandon them.

"Artemis!" Tilly shouted, not wanting to leave her alone. "We have to go! Are you okay?" Tilly wasn't really expecting a response at this stage; the air around Artemis was shimmering and jolting, almost like a glitching video game. And then she opened her eyes and stared right at them, with a look that could only be described as triumphant.

"Thank you," she said, her voice airy and unsubstantial. "I will not forget your help. I hope that I will see you in your imaginations." And then she closed her eyes again as her body started to fade, sparkling particles drifting away into the air as dust rained down on them from the shaking roof.

"Thank you!" Tilly said, starting to cry from the loss and the fear and the uncertainty, before being tugged away by Alessia, who was staring over Tilly's shoulder at the space where Artemis had been.

"Come on!" Alessia yelled, her attention now focused on the rapidly disintegrating Archive. The three of them *darted through* the door back into the corridor, heading in the direction of the main entrance, but slabs of masonry were falling in bigger and bigger pieces, and it was hard even to stay on their feet. They dodged and weaved as best they could, but Tilly felt a sharp pain scratch at her arm as a painting dislodged from the wall and *fell against* her. She was barely holding on to the Records, and she could see Milo was struggling too.

They were only meters from the entrance when a crash echoed through the air and a great swathe of the wall descended in front of them, blocking their way to the door, dust and bricks spilling out onto the carpet.

"Come on, this way!" Milo shouted, gesturing with his

head to a gap left by the demolished wall, where the bleak gardens of the Archive could be seen, and beyond them the gates to the Quip. Milo started trying to scramble over the bricks without dropping the Records, but Tilly spun round, making sure Alessia had heard and was following too.

"Alessia!" she yelled, not able to see her.

"I'm here," a weak voice said. "By the wall."

Tilly looked to the ground, and there was Alessia, her face even paler than usual.

Her foot was stuck fast under a pile of bricks, and there was a thin trickle of blood on her cheek.

43

Floating in Story

"**M**ilo!" Tilly called. "Stop, wait! Alessia's stuck . . . she's hurt. Oh no, oh no. What do we do?"

This wasn't a situation they could read themselves out of or research in a book. This was real bricks and blood, and she had no idea what to try. She started digging through the pile of rubble, trying to work out which bricks she could move without risking the heap of stone falling onto both of them. The ground was shaking more and more violently underneath them, and the piles of debris kept moving and shifting.

"Go without me," Alessia said quietly.

"Don't be daft," Milo said, as he put his Records down next to Tilly's and helped with the rubble.

"We've nearly got you," Tilly said, brushing dust from her face.

All they could do was concentrate on getting Alessia's foot

free as quickly as they could, trying to block out the chaos and the noise of the Archive falling down around them.

But Alessia's foot was still stuck fast—all they had managed to do was remove enough of the stone so that they could see more of her leg, down to her ankle, which was twisted at an angle that made Tilly feel a little queasy. As well as the physical destruction around them, the walls had now started to spark and glitter and fade as though they were evaporating away.

"Maybe the rocks trapping Alessia will disappear?" Milo said hopefully.

"But then there won't be anything left!" Tilly said, her head spinning. "We'll just be floating in Story, or we'll vanish with it, or . . . or . . ."

"Some of your dad's elixir would come in handy right now," Milo said, but Alessia didn't hear him as she'd passed out from the pain. Tilly quickly checked her pulse, and to her relief Alessia was definitely still breathing.

"Oh no, oh no," Tilly said again, more scared than she'd ever felt before. "What do we do, Milo?"

"We just have to keep trying," he said, determination across his worried face. "It's all we can do, right? We just have to try and get her out until we manage or the whole place disappears."

Tilly nodded and they kept

going, but the rocks were either stuck fast or far too big for them to move. There was a huge beam of wood keeping everything in place, which Alessia's foot was wedged under. But they kept trying.

As they did so, neither noticed that when she'd fallen, Alessia's backpack had crashed to the ground, spilling its contents and smashing the glass jug. Behind them, the remnants of the powder dispersed into a cloud of glittering motes of *book magic* that swirled in the air before settling gently onto Tilly and Milo as they worked.

44

The Most Important Job

Tilly wiped a filthy hand across her forehead, and it came away . . . sparkling? She stared at it for a second before chalking it up to the *book magic* escaping as the Archive collapsed around them. Everything felt overwhelming and useless—but they had no other option but to keep trying. She tried not to think about her family, who would probably be waking up and realizing she wasn't there at any moment, and in particular she tried not to think about the sleeping face of her grandad, who she was not going to manage to wake up. Everything they'd done and learned was going to be for nothing.

And then.

"Oh, the poor thing!" a voice said from behind them, making both Tilly and Milo jump. They spun round to see four children standing there, all gently glittering round the edges.

"Anne?!" Tilly said, jumping to her feet and throwing her arms round Anne Shirley in all of her red-headed goodness.

"Matilda!" Anne said in delight. "Why on earth are we here? Is that girl okay?"

"No, she's not," Tilly said. "And I don't know why you're here—and, wait . . ." She turned. "Who are *you*?" She looked more closely at the other three children.

"It's . . . it's you," Milo said, confused. "It's Bobbie and Peter and Phyllis. It's the Railway Children. What are you doing here?"

"I assure you I have no idea," Peter said, looking rather put out to have been yanked away from whatever he was doing. Bobbie was already kneeling by Alessia, smoothing her hair away from her damp forehead and assessing her condition. Phyllis just looked a little awestruck at the sight of the sparkling, crumbling Archive.

"I suppose we were needed," Anne said cheerfully, taking the whole situation in her stride. Tilly stared at her and then looked down at her sparkling skin in wonder. Her skin felt as though it was gently charged, and she looked over to see that Milo was the same.

"Comfort blanket characters," she breathed to herself in amazement. She was suffused with *book magic*, and it was beautiful. She felt all the stories that had built her, and all the stories she'd left a trace of herself in. Her Record might be a physical manifestation of her reading life, but it was all inside her heart and her mind, all the time, for when she needed it. And *Anne of Green Gables* was at its core, just as *The Railway Children* was for Milo. Anne did always turn up when she was most needed, and Tilly felt that familiar burst of courage that she always pulled from Anne Shirley. It was time to rescue Alessia and get to the Quip.

"How is she, Bobbie?" Peter asked his sister.

"She'll be okay," Bobbie said, looking up from Alessia. "She's just fainted, and if we get her out, I think her ankle will heal—I don't believe it's been crushed. It's just stuck under this beam."

"Right then," Peter said, rolling up his sleeves and immediately taking charge. Tilly noticed Anne rolling her eyes. "Bobbie, you stay with—what's her name?"

"Alessia," Milo supplied.

"Okay, Bobbie, you stay with Alessia. Make sure she is as safe as can be; Milo and I will—"

"You know my name?" Milo said in disbelief.

"Of course we do," Peter replied. "Don't be a dolt—come and help me move this beam."

"It shouldn't just be the boys who move it!" Anne said, disgruntled. "Let me help too!"

"Fine," Peter said. "Just don't get in the way. You take this end with me, and, Milo, you take that end with . . . ?"

"Tilly."

"Right, with Tilly, get as good a hold of the edges as you can."

"What about me?" Phyllis said plaintively. "Let me help!"

"You have the most important job," Peter said to Phyllis. "You have to watch the rest of the rubble as we move the beam and shout if you see anything falling. Can you do that?"

"Yes," Phyllis said with determination, and stood with her arms crossed, glaring at the heap of detritus.

"How did he know my name?" Milo said to Tilly as they tried to get a firm grip on the corners of the huge wooden beam.

"I think it's because they're not from the books," Tilly said. "They're from you. From your memories. The characters you carry around with you all the time. I think they're our comfort blanket characters." Tilly saw the same understanding settle on him that she'd just felt wash over her.

"Wow," he said, and despite the precariousness of the situation, he couldn't keep the smile from his face as Peter did a countdown and the four of them heaved with all of their might.

The beam moved, but only barely.

"All safe, Phyllis?" Peter shouted, and she nodded.

"Yes, keep going!"

"All safe, Bobbie?"

"Just the same," Bobbie said, arching her body over Alessia's to protect her from anything that might fall.

"Once more!" Peter yelled, and again the four of them hauled with as much strength as they could muster. This time it moved decisively.

"Hold it! Hold it!" Peter said. "Bobbie! Drag her out! Phyllis, help your sister!"

Tilly could feel her arms shaking under the weight of the beam and saw sweat dripping down Milo's face with the effort of keeping it up and from crashing down onto Bobbie and Phyllis, who were gently pulling Alessia out from underneath.

"I can't hold it much longer!" Anne said, her face red and strained with the effort.

"Me . . . neither . . ." Peter grunted.

"She's out!" Bobbie shouted, as she and Phyllis got Alessia clear of the rubble.

"Right, on my count, we drop it at the same time and run," Peter said. "Make sure you have a clear direction to move in so the beam doesn't fall on your feet." The other three silently nodded. "One! Two! Three!"

Tilly let the beam slip from her aching fingers and darted out of its way as it crashed down, bringing more rubble and dust as it fell. It slammed into the ground, smashing the wood to pieces and indenting itself into the floor. The four of them who had been holding the beam up sagged against the crumbling, shaking walls, getting their breath back.

"I say, well done, everyone," Peter said, giving Anne a firm pat on the back.

"Well done for having a plan," she said fairly. "You were very calm under pressure."

"Thanks," Peter said gruffly.

"We need to get going," Tilly said, breathing heavily. "We have to get back to the Quip. Bobbie, can you help me carry Alessia? It's not very far, and at least once we get into the garden we'll be safer from falling bits."

They gathered around Bobbie, who had Alessia's head in her lap. Alessia's ankle was nastily swollen and bleeding but still very much attached. She started to murmur as she came to.

"What . . . what's happening?" she said, her face white. "Where are we?"

"We're still in the Archive," Tilly said. "These are some friends; they're going to help us all get back to the Quip. Bobbie, can you take her other arm and we can lift her together?"

Bobbie nodded and gently laid Alessia's head down as she got to her feet. Between them they lifted Alessia as carefully as they could, although Tilly could see how much pain she was in—she was clenching her jaw tightly and there were tears leaking out of the corners of her eyes, but she didn't let out any sounds or complain at all. They arranged her with one arm over

Bobbie's shoulders and one arm over Tilly's, and the unlikely group somehow got through the gap in the collapsed wall and out into the garden.

"Okay, nearly there," Milo breathed, walking ahead. "The gates aren't far. Shall I go and get the Quip unlocked?"

"Yes," Tilly said, breathing heavily, and Milo raced off ahead.

"Let me take over," Anne said, seeing her exhaustion, and Tilly gratefully transferred Alessia's weight over to her, with Peter taking over from Bobbie. They were moving more slowly than Tilly would have liked, but there was no way they could go faster. They hadn't got far through the gardens when an almighty rumbling, greater than anything they had heard before, echoed through the sky.

Turning round, the group stopped for a moment in awe as what was left of the Archive finally collapsed completely. It thundered down now, huge chunks of masonry toppling, with billows of dust shooting up into the air, and glass shattering from windows.

The whole place was giving off sparks of *book magic* and shimmering in and out of existence as it fell. An explosion shook the watchers out of their trance, and flames started to lick their way up the destroyed remains of the wing where the Archive had been.

Tilly gave a gasp of horror.

"The Records," she said. "We've left the Records."

"What are the Records?" Anne asked. "Can we help?"

"Did you see the white books?" Tilly said. "We had some piles of white books with us before Alessia got trapped, and we need them to save my grandad."

She turned desperately to look at what was left of the building, which was being taken over by fire and smoke. All the hope and adrenaline drained out of her abruptly. Everything they'd worked for and done, gone just like that; there was no way to wake up Grandad or Horatio now.

"We'll get them," Peter said solemnly. "You take Alessia with Bobbie, and Anne and I will go and find them. You left them where the beam fell?"

"Yes, but I can't ask you to do that," Tilly said. "It's too dangerous."

"Will you come with me, Anne?" Peter said. "I can tell you're brave enough."

"Of course," Anne said, wiping a dirty hand on her pinafore and flicking her red braids behind her shoulder. "Let's go."

"Are you sure?"

"I've never been surer," Anne said, giving Tilly a one-armed hug before they transferred Alessia back to Bobbie and Tilly. Alessia tried to put weight on her foot but let out an involuntary cry of pain as it touched the ground. The three of them and Phyllis started edging their way toward the gates to the train station as Peter and Anne ran back toward the burning building.

45

One More Moment

It seemed like it took an eternity to get to the broken golden gates, but finally there was Milo, standing anxiously by the train, whistle in hand.

"Where are the others?" he called.

"They've gone back for the Records!" Tilly said as they stumbled toward him.

"The Records," Milo said softly, clearly having the same horrible realization as Tilly had had. The whole reason they had come here, until the priority became saving Alessia.

"Don't worry—I'm sure Peter and Anne will find them," Bobbie said as she unhooked Alessia's arm from round her neck. Between them, they got Alessia up the stairs into the carriage where she sat, propped up against the wall, a grimace of pain on her face.

"How long do we leave it before we go?" asked Milo, his face furrowed with worry.

"It's the only way we have to wake up Grandad," Tilly said, as she and Milo climbed back down to the platform. "We have to wait, and now we're at the Quip we can wait a bit longer because . . . Oh no."

"What?" Bobbie said, scanning the gates for her brother.

"Look," Tilly said, gesturing at the horizon.

They could no longer see the smoke and fire of the Archive burning, or anything at all beyond the gates, just a hazy dark mist that was floating in the air—no, not floating, but moving closer toward them.

"Everything is disappearing," Milo said.

"What about Peter?" Phyllis said in a small voice.

"I'm sure he's coming," Tilly said, but she wasn't sure at all. She had no idea how these versions of Anne and the Railway Children worked; they weren't like the normal characters from the books. They were *their* versions, from their memories and hearts. If the Archive disintegrated while Peter and Anne were there, would they vanish too? She'd seen the way people's memories evaporated when Source Editions were destroyed. Who would she even be if she'd never read *Anne of Green Gables*?

"It's coming apart at the seams," Tilly said in horror. "There's so much book magic here, but nothing holding it together anymore. No Archivists, no rules, no bookwanderers, and now, no Artemis."

"Story is claiming it back," Alessia said weakly from inside the carriage. And Tilly realized she was right. The black mist was Story itself; it was just like the view out of the windows of the Quip as they traveled. She just had never seen it move like this; on the Quip it was like traveling through inky, beautiful space, but this . . . this felt like an almost living thing, moving and thinking and reclaiming.

"We're going to have to go," Tilly said, feeling sick at the thought.

"One more moment," Milo said.

"We can't leave them!" Bobbie cried, running back toward the gates. Phyllis followed her without thinking, and the second their feet left the Quip, the cobblestones of the platform started dissolving away, leaving a chasm of darkness with Bobbie and Phyllis on one side by the gates and the Quip on the other.

"Will they be okay?" Milo said, staring at the girls. "Can we leave them? It'll be fine, right? They're from our memories, they can't get hurt?"

"I don't know," Tilly said. "I hope so, but I don't know what happens if they vanish into *book magic*, it might be like the Source Editions being destroyed."

"No, no, that can't happen," Milo said desperately. "I can't lose them. We can't go."

"I don't know what options we have left," Tilly said, feeling as wretched as Milo sounded. To have got so close to saving Grandad, and to stumble at the last hurdle, as well as risk losing Anne, was too much to bear. Milo turned to go back up into the carriage, unable to look at Bobbie and Phyllis, who were stuck helplessly on a patch of platform by the gates, the chasm growing larger and larger with every passing second.

"I'm so sorry," Tilly called to them, feeling useless and ashamed. But as she turned to follow Milo, the unmistakable sound of footsteps echoed into the emptiness.

"*Waiiiiit!*" a voice yelled.

46

I Always Knew
the Railway Was Enchanted
(Reprise)

In a rush of grimy limbs and paper, Peter and Anne hurtled through the gates, each holding a pile of Records, which were now dirty and covered in soot, as were Anne and Peter.

"We found them," Peter said triumphantly, but pulled up short when he saw the great vast darkness separating what was left of the Archive from the slice of train tracks that the Quip was hanging on to. There was no longer any solid ground, just the tracks, with Tilly was standing on the bottom step, precariously close to the edge. And behind Peter, his sisters, and Anne, the gates themselves had started to fizz and vanish so that the four book characters looked as though they were standing on a column in the middle of the night sky, with *book magic* crackling and sparkling around them.

"Can you catch?" Anne shouted across to her, eyeing up the gap.

"I can try," Tilly said. "There's nothing else for it!"

"One at a time!" Peter said, passing his pile to Bobbie. He took the top Record, lined himself up with Tilly, and threw it. It sliced into the air, pages fluttering, and Tilly held her arms out, making herself focus on its arc and keeping her eyes on the book. It landed heavily in her arms. She felt slightly winded, but that was nothing in comparison to the relief of catching it. She chucked it behind her into the carriage.

"Next one!" she called, and this time Anne took one of her pile and carefully aimed and threw it. But, as they threw the Records across, the ground they were all on was vanishing steadily, and soon the four characters were clumped together on a tiny outcrop, Phyllis clinging desperately onto Bobbie.

"There's just one more!" Anne said. She looked at the spine. "It's your grandad's, Tilly!"

"Milo, are we ready to go?" Tilly called, and Milo stuck his head out of the engine cab.

"Whenever you say," he said, breathing heavily.

"Ready?" Peter shouted, and Tilly nodded.

Peter threw her grandad's Record up into the air, and the book sailed across the darkness, but he'd not got the angle quite right. There wasn't space where he was standing to throw it with enough force, and Tilly could see that the book wasn't going to make it.

She leaned forward, holding on to the metal rail on the train with one arm, tilting out into the emptiness.

Everything felt like it was happening in slow motion as the pages fluttered and the book came *toward* her, all of her grandad's reading life—and the last thing she needed to be able to save him—soaring through Story.

She felt the book brush against her fingertips, but it was too heavy and too far for her to catch at this angle. She cried out in frustration and leaned out until only the very edges of her fingers were still holding on to the rail, and she had it! Her hand closed around its spine and she had it!

But no, the momentum was too much and there was no way for her to swing herself back, and the book was still too heavy, and she could feel herself slipping. And then, a strong hand on her wrist and a weight behind her, and she was being pulled back into the Quip. She fell backward, on top of Alessia, who had dragged herself to the door and saved Tilly.

"I've got you," she said. "But please could you get off my foot?" She grimaced in pain.

Tilly rolled off her and put her grandad's Record on the floor before leaning out the door again.

"Milo," she called upward. "We can go. We've got them all." She stared out at Anne, Bobbie, Peter, and Phyllis, who were all crushed together on the tiny stretch of stone still left.

But then, just before it disappeared completely, they started to glow. At the same moment, Tilly felt her skin start to prickle, and she stared down to see the remnants of the Alchemist's elixir on her hands, the dark powder shimmering with *book magic*. Coils of magic sprang from her, and she looked up to see Anne waving and grinning at her, as gentle tendrils of *book magic* enveloped the four characters.

As Tilly leaned out of the Quip, holding that last glimpse of Anne in her mind, she saw Milo poking his head out of the engine cab, waving wildly at the characters as the *book magic* came to take them home again.

"Bye, Peter!" he called, and

Tilly could hear that he was fighting back tears. "Bye, Phyllis! Bye, Bobbie! Thank you!"

"Good-bye, Milo!" came the reply. Peter gave a sharp salute with a grin, Phyllis waved madly as she held her sister's hand, and Bobbie blew a kiss as they started to fade.

"True friends are always together in spirit!" Anne called as the Quip rumbled forward, and the last thing Tilly heard was Phyllis's voice, echoing into the sparkling darkness.

"I always knew the railway was *enchanted*."

47

More Secrets

Once they were safely on their way, the three of them sat, exhausted and overwhelmed, in Horatio's office. Milo had found some painkillers for Alessia in Horatio's desk, and after they'd cleaned her wound it looked considerably less scary than Tilly had feared. The three of them, however, were still all covered in scratches and blood, as well as dust and dirt.

"So, the Archive and Artemis are just gone now?" Tilly asked, feeling a sense of loss wash over her. She wondered if Story was done with her now that the Archive was destroyed or if her abilities would change or disappear. Maybe this would finally put a stop to her unpredictable bookwandering, once and for all.

"It's strange to think of all those Records that just don't exist now," Milo said sadly. "But at least Artemis was happy."

"She looked elated," Alessia said, wincing as she moved

herself into a more comfortable position. "I was so scared when she started gasping and choking, but I suppose it was never going to work the same on her as my father. I just hope she's at peace, wherever she went."

"Alessia, can we finish the cure now that we have the Records?" Tilly asked. "While we're on the way home? Artemis said that when a Record burns, it releases the *book magic* inside—so do we just burn a bit of my grandad's and add it to the cure?"

"I . . . guess so?" Alessia said.

"I hope so," Tilly said. "And you're sure you're happy to use the vial you took from the Alchemist for Grandad, Milo?"

"I'm sure," Milo said. "We'll be able to make more with Alessia's recipe, and we have Horatio's Record, so let's get Archie better first. He'll probably be able to help us find the ingredients we need anyway. If we're lucky, some of them might even be in the compendium."

Tilly glanced at Alessia, who had a strange look on her face, but Tilly was too focused on getting the cure finished to worry about it. She fished the box of matches out of Alessia's backpack and picked up her grandad's Record. It was huge. A life full of stories and adventure and bookwandering. She didn't look too closely, though, as it felt so personal; she just ripped out a page without looking and hoped that would work.

Milo had fetched a tin plate from the pantry, and Tilly carefully struck the match and set light to one corner of the paper. It quickly caught and curled black as the fire spread. Tilly dropped it onto the plate, where it flickered and burned and then went out, leaving a charred piece of paper.

"Do you have the vial ready?" she asked Milo, who went to get the box from Horatio's desk where they'd left it. He very delicately took out the glass vial and unstopped it, holding it out to Tilly, who picked up a pinch of the ash from the burned paper and sprinkled it in.

Milo pushed the stopper on firmly and gave the vial a gentle shake. A shimmer of rainbow light flickered across it, and then it was back to its deep-purple color.

"Is that it?" Tilly said to Alessia. "Will it work?"

"I think so," Alessia said, sounding resigned. "My father made that dose, and all it needed was the last ingredient."

Tilly sagged in relief. "Thank you so much, Alessia," she said. "I can't tell you how grateful my family are going to be; everyone is going to be so excited to meet you."

Alessia gave a small smile. "How long will it take to get there?" she asked.

"Not too long," Milo said. "An hour or so? We should probably rest or eat or something."

But before they could do any of that there was a bright ringing sound, almost like a doorbell.

"What now?" Tilly said, half weary, half scared.

"Oh, don't worry—it's just the post," Milo said.

"How on earth does the post get here?" Tilly said. "It

never worked when Oskar and I tried to write to you via the Endpapers—we sent loads of notes and letters by the back of books, but we never heard from you."

"I swear I never got them. I wasn't ignoring you, I promise! It *does* work usually; it's how Horatio gets requests from clients, and I suppose it's also how he communicated with the Alchemist. I guess he just didn't bother passing on any notes from you. And, let's be honest, he was probably reading them too. I hope you didn't say anything you didn't mind him knowing."

"I think he'd have probably found them extremely boring," Tilly said, grinning to think of all the letters she and Oskar had posted and how tiresome Horatio must have found it to read through their jokes and stories and questions.

"Let's go check what this is then," Milo said, standing up and going over to a metal panel on the wall of the carriage, which he unlocked with his uncle's keys and slid upward using a narrow handle at the bottom. Underneath was, improbably, a copper-colored tray underneath a letterbox. In the tray were several letters, which Milo scooped up and brought over.

"Oh, look!" he said, delighted. "This *is* from you! It's the note you sent to tell me to come back and meet you at midnight!"

There were two more items of post, and one was on thick creamy paper with a wax stamp with an all-too-familiar symbol stamped into it.

"From my father," Alessia said.

"Do you want to read it?" Milo asked, but she shook her

head, so Milo slit open the wax seal and unfolded the paper. "It's for you," he said to Tilly, and passed it over.

"'Dear Matilda,'" she read aloud.

Dear Matilda,

I was very disappointed both in your decision and the manner of your leaving. I have no doubt that my daughter has filled your heads with lies about my intentions, which are exactly as I set out to you, but no matter. Please know that the offer still stands. If you retrieve The Book of Books from the Botanist for me, I will exchange it for the cure for your grandfather. Due to the escalation of the situation, I also will offer to ensure the ongoing safety of both you and Milo Bolt, regardless of the terms of my previous contract with Horatio. But please understand that if you choose not to cooperate you risk the well-being of the rest of your family—and you know that I am not a man of empty threats. I look forward to seeing you in Venice again soon, with the book.

Yours,
Geronimo della Porta

Tilly felt sick. He was threatening her grandma and her mum now, not to mention offering to protect Milo as some sort of treacherous bargain.

"He's lying," Alessia said. "You cannot trust anything he says. All he wants is the book."

"I can't risk my family," Tilly said. "Not after everything we've done to save Grandad. What's the other letter, Milo? Is it from him too?"

"No," Milo said slowly as he scanned the other piece of paper. His eyes widened. "I think it's from the Botanist—it talks about the poisons."

Horatio,

I hope you are well. Please provide me with an update on your progress in discovering the poison compendium I inquired about. You know that we cannot continue with our work to stop the Alchemist without its contents. I know that your mother is also eager to see you; it has been too long since you visited.

Best,
R

"Your grandmother is with the Botanist?" Tilly said, shocked. "I thought she was dead—how else could Horatio be the driver?"

"More secrets," Milo said. "We know she wasn't in the hot air balloon accident, but the Alchemist said something about her being in disgrace, maybe *because* of the accident? I don't know . . . I guess I hadn't realized how much I was hoping she might still be alive until I saw this . . ."

"And 'R' is definitely the Botanist," Tilly said. "Artemis told me that her real name is Rosa."

"But, more importantly, it says that she and your uncle are working together to stop my father," Alessia said. "And you have this compendium already?" Tilly and Milo nodded. "Well then, we need to take it to her—we should do that first."

"No!" Tilly said in horror. "We have to go and wake up Grandad first—what are you talking about?"

"And Tilly's family will be able to help us," Milo said. "We can make a proper plan at Pages & Co., but don't worry, we're all on the same side. We'll make sure we speak to the Botanist."

"And you know where she is?" Alessia said.

"Yes," Milo said. "In Northumberland. I've never actually been off the Quip there, but I know the place we stop, and it's easy to imagine once you've seen it. It's right by Hadrian's Wall, in a dip between two hills where there's a sycamore tree. I can picture it."

"Don't picture it too hard," Tilly said anxiously. "We don't want to divert there before we've been home."

"Don't worry," Milo said, sounding exhausted. "I think I've just about got the hang of this driving thing now; we're definitely heading to *Pages & Co.* first. Since your grandma has been taking care of your grandad for a few weeks now, I was hoping she might look at Horatio too and make sure he's doing okay. We haven't given him any water or anything, and he's been unconscious for the whole night now."

"I'm sure she will," Tilly said, feeling her heart start to race as she thought of seeing her grandma and mum—and worrying a little bit about having to explain to them where she'd snuck off to. But she had the cure, she had done it. They had done it. They were going to save Grandad.

MILO

48

A Lot of Explaining to Do

"**H**ere we are then," Milo said, as he felt the Quip starting to slow down.

The closer they had got to Pages & Co., the more unsettled he felt. The idea of the Pageses' warm and welcoming kitchen was drawing him on, but the inevitable switch that was about to happen, from the three of them as a team to Tilly being absorbed back into her family, made him feel on shaky ground. He could see that Alessia clearly felt very nervous about arriving too. Tilly's family may have a complicated past, but they loved each other so much. Alessia didn't even know her mother, and her father was an evil genius, which had to take its toll, Milo thought.

And then there was him. Milo had never really thought about whether he loved his uncle; it seemed an absurd thing to contemplate. But Horatio was the only family he knew, and it seemed as though, in many ways, everything he had done was to protect Milo, which was some sort of love, he supposed.

As it did last time, the Quip managed to curl up among the bookshelves like a sleepy cat, and Milo opened the door into the dark bookshop. The clock on the wall showed that it was seven thirty a.m., and morning light was spilling in through the windows. The books were lit up in the hopeful, fresh glow of a summer sunrise.

"Come on!" Tilly called excitedly, her eyes alight at being home. She grabbed Milo's hand and tried to yank him forward, toward the door to the kitchen.

"I need to help Alessia," Milo said. "You go on."

And Tilly didn't need telling twice, running ahead and swinging the door open. Milo heard shouts of delight and relief echo outward: clearly Tilly's absence had already been noted, even though she had barely been gone at all in the end. He and Alessia slowly and carefully walked toward the warmth of the kitchen, Alessia leaning heavily on Milo's arm because of her ankle. Milo found that he was suddenly very glad that she was there.

As soon as they stepped into the kitchen, they were set upon by a torrent of hugs and kisses and affection. Elsie immediately had Alessia sitting on a kitchen chair, her foot raised on another, and was rooting through a first-aid box. Bea was holding Tilly tightly, concern etched on her brow as she took in her daughter's scratches and tangled hair. Milo stood to one side, not knowing what to do with himself. He was handed a huge mug of hot chocolate, and a plate of toast appeared on the table. Alessia gave Milo a small smile from where she was sitting, and he tried to smile back, but for some reason there were tears threatening to escape. And so he just drank his hot chocolate instead, not even noticing that it was burning his tongue.

"Right, then," Elsie said, once they were all settled. "Clearly, there is an awful lot you need to tell us and a *lot* of explaining to do."

"Never mind that," Tilly started.

"Never mind you sneaking off in the middle of the night even though we expressly told Horatio we were not taking his deal?" Elsie said, with a raised eyebrow.

"Yes! Never mind any of that!" Tilly said, fizzing up and down with excitement. "Because we have it, Grandma! We got it; we found the cure!"

Elsie sat down heavily on a kitchen chair, her cheeks very flushed. "Are you sure it works?" she asked quietly.

"Almost totally," Tilly said. "But it was all of us who found it—and we would never have known how to complete it if it wasn't for Alessia. And she knows how to make more so we can wake Horatio up!"

Alessia gave a weak smile.

"Well, what are we waiting for?" Bea said. "Come on, Mum. Let's wake him up."

Milo stayed seated, not wanting to intrude on the private moment.

"If you think you two aren't part of this, then you're dafter than I gave you credit for," Elsie said. "It's clear Tilly couldn't have done any of this without you. Come on, come upstairs."

"Alessia won't be able to get up the stairs," Milo said. "I should stay with her."

"Well, all right then," Elsie said. "Although I'm sure Archie will want to say thank you as soon as he comes to." But she was eager to go and save her husband and didn't insist again that they came upstairs.

After Elsie, Bea, and Tilly had gone in a clatter of excitement, Alessia turned to Milo.

"I need to tell you something," she said, looking ill.

"What?"

"I don't know how to make more of the cure," she admitted. "I'm so sorry."

"You lied to us?" Milo said, staring at her in disbelief.

"No, not really, not properly," Alessia said. "I *do* have the recipe. It's just that I have no idea what lots of the ingredients are or where to find them. And the ones I do know about are really difficult to find; it's not as simple as just going to a pharmacy or a supermarket or a garden. They're hidden in books and libraries and all sorts of places."

"Right," Milo said quietly, taking it in. "But . . . but what about my uncle?"

"I'm so sorry, Milo," Alessia said, close to tears. "But I needed you to help me escape. You've no idea what it's like living with him. I needed you both to leave and take me with you—but I wasn't actually lying about anything! He really would have killed you if you'd stayed, and he wouldn't have ever sent the cure here. I have the list of ingredients, all of them, I swear. Only . . . it's not going to be easy to find them."

"But what . . ." He stopped, as from upstairs there came an almighty cheer. "I guess it worked," he said. "At least you got that right."

"I'm sorry," Alessia said again.

"I know," Milo said, and he did know. He understood what it was like to be lonely and to live without friends or family who really saw you. Alessia's situation was far more dangerous, but he felt his life had more in common with hers than with Tilly's. Before he learned that Horatio was trying to protect him, he would have jumped at the chance to escape the Quip. At the same time, he felt all mixed up about Alessia hiding the truth from him and Tilly and didn't know what to say to her.

He was saved from having to work it out by noisy footsteps coming back downstairs, and the kitchen door swung open to reveal a crying Elsie and Bea, a pink-faced, delighted Tilly, and an exhausted, pale but definitely awake Archie.

"I hear you two are to thank for this," he said, and his voice was shaky and made him seem much older than he was. He held a hand out to shake, and when Milo took it he enclosed Milo's hand in his other.

"Thank you, Milo," he said. "We owe you an eternal debt of gratitude. And you too! Alessia, I think? It sounds like you've risked an awful lot to save an old man you don't know. Thank you."

Alessia just gave a wobbly smile, which was easily explained to the others by the discomfort of her ankle.

Elsie guided Archie to a chair and tucked a blanket over his knees before getting a large glass of water for him.

"Now, Milo," she said. "Tilly said your uncle has been poisoned as well. You did an incredibly selfless thing by letting Tilly take the dose of the cure for Archie, and we'll do anything we can to help you, although it sounds like we have most of what we need thanks to Alessia."

Alessia burst into tears.

"We don't have . . . quite as much as we hoped," Milo said, not making eye contact with Alessia. "Alessia has the recipe, but it would seem the ingredients are a little harder to find than we thought."

"Well, you have all of us, and Amelia, to help now," Elsie said. "We can give the recipe to the Underlibrarians right away tomorrow, and they'll get started. But for now shall we get your uncle off your train and into a bed so we can take better care of him?"

Milo nodded gratefully.

Bea stayed with Alessia in the kitchen, while Elsie went with Milo and Tilly to Horatio's carriage. Milo unlocked the door, and the three of them climbed up to where Horatio lay on his bed, looking as though he were simply sleeping, apart from his purple fingertips.

"Just like Archie," Elsie said sadly, seeing the stains. "Okay, now if I take his arms, will you each take one of his legs, and try not to bang his head on the door as we go."

It was an awkward procession, and Milo was glad Horatio would not remember his rather undignified arrival at *Pages & Co.* Once they were back in the kitchen, Bea got involved too, and between the four of them they managed to get him up the first flight of stairs and into a bedroom.

"Try not to worry too much," Elsie said, putting a gentle arm round Milo's shoulders. "We've taken care of Archie for over two weeks now, and look how he's doing. With some good food and plenty of care, he'll be back to normal in no time. We'll make sure that your uncle is looked after until we can wake him up."

Once Horatio was installed in a freshly made bed, they all reconvened round the kitchen table. But, as they quizzed Alessia and asked for more details on the recipe and ingredients, and as Tilly explained what they'd learned about the Alchemist and the Botanist, Milo felt more and more anxious and overwhelmed.

"Don't you think we should go straight to the Botanist?" he

said, but his suggestion was lost in the friendly chatter of the Pages family, all speaking affectionately over each other as they bounced ideas around. Elsie and Archie wanted to go to the Underlibrary and start some serious research into the cure but also into all of the Alchemist's recipes and schemes from Alessia's notebook.

"My uncle and the Botanist already have a plan," Milo pointed out.

"The thing is, with Horatio asleep, it's hard to factor that in right now," Elsie said kindly.

"But we need to take the poisons to the Botanist," Milo said. "My uncle wouldn't have said that with his last words if it wasn't important. We already got off track once because I didn't understand, but that's what we need to do. And I'm sure the Botanist could help us find some of the ingredients for the cure."

"Milo's right," Tilly agreed. "That's what she collects books about after all."

"We just don't know anything about her," Elsie said. "However we can absolutely reach out to her—I'm sure Amelia will have some record of her at the Underlibrary; we can get her going on that tomorrow. But it's too much of a risk before we know who she is. And Milo, sweetheart, your uncle had rather unusual methods, and not all of them safe."

Milo couldn't really argue with that.

But there was one other thing he couldn't ignore, one thing that everyone else had seemed to forget about—that his grandmother was with the Botanist. Finding out what had happened to

Evalina wasn't going to be a priority for anyone who was focused on stopping the Alchemist, and Milo understood why that was right. But it was what he had to know. He needed to save his uncle and find his grandmother, and the Botanist was where to start, especially as she was working against the Alchemist too. It seemed so obvious to him, but as the conversation went on, he felt more and more on the edge of it. And, despite the fact that it was his family tangled up in it all, he felt less and less useful.

He glanced over at Alessia and saw that she was watching quietly too. It was her father causing so many of these problems after all: she must be desperate to help properly, and she must know so much that was useful. Meanwhile, the Pages family were locked in their debate about what to do, talking in easy, familiar family shorthand and referencing people and things that Milo had no idea about.

There was a cough from across the table, and he looked up to see that Alessia was trying to catch his eye. Her cough hadn't interrupted the flow of the Pageses' family discussion, and so she raised an eyebrow and nodded her head toward the door. Milo looked back at Tilly and her family and nodded his head in response.

"We're just going to go and get some stuff from the Quip," he said, standing up.

"Okay, dear," Elsie said, barely breaking off from the conversation. Milo helped Alessia stand up, and the noise attracted Tilly's attention.

"Do you need me to come and help?" she asked.

"We're okay," he replied. "You stay here with your family."
Tilly gave him a huge smile, and with that Milo and Alessia left
the warmth and the light of the kitchen for the bright and empty
bookshop and the Quip.

"We're going to just have to get on with it ourselves, right?"
Alessia said.

"I think we have to," he replied. "We should leave a note
though, to let them know where we're going and that we'll be back.
We need to start with the Botanist and take her the poison box."

"And you need to find out if your grandmother is there,"
Alessia said. "I understand. And I'm truly sorry I wasn't completely honest about the cure."

"I know," Milo said. "I've already forgiven you."

Milo quickly wrote a note for Tilly and her family on a
piece of notepaper and left it on the front desk at *Pages & Co.*
for them to find easily.

Dear Tilly,

*We've gone to find the Botanist. We'll be back when we
have the cure and some answers. You know how to write
to us, so stay in touch.*

See you soon,
Milo and Alessia

Milo knew that it was time for him and Alessia to slip quickly and quietly away. He took one last look at the kitchen door over his shoulder, but they had everything they needed.

He helped Alessia up into the Quip and followed after her, closing the carriage door. This was their story now.

— THE END —

Acknowledgments

Thank you to my agent Claire Wilson for your wisdom, kindness, and friendship, and to everyone at RCW, in particular Safae El-Ouahabi and David Dunn.

Thank you to my publisher, HarperCollins Children's Books, for taking such good care of Pages & Co. Thank you to my editor, Nick Lake, for your insight and thoughtfulness, to Julia Sanderson for being a savior on a regular basis due to your amazing brain, and to Louisa Sheridan—you are the most wonderful, fun, smart publicist an author could dream of. Thank you also to Ann-Janine Murtagh, Samantha Stewart, Jo-Anna Parkinson, Jess Dean, Elisa Offord, Beth Maher, Alex Cowan, Elorine Grant, Francesca Lecchini-Lee, Carla Alonzi, Laure Gysemans, Elizabeth Vaziri and Mary Finch; I know that so much goes into publishing books that I don't see, and I am so appreciative of everyone at HCCB.

Thank you always to Lizzie Clifford, Sarah Hughes, and Rachel Denwood.

Thank you to my foreign publishers; your support and enthusiasm in helping Pages find readers means the world. In particular thank you to Cheryl Eissing, Tessa Meischeid, and the team at Philomel Books.

Thank you so much to Marco Guadalupi for your utterly beautiful illustrations, and for capturing the world of Pages & Co. so magically, and thank you to Paola Escobar for your work on the first three books.

Thank you to Edward Brooke-Hitching for your book, *The Madman's Library*, which is where I read about the real-life sixteenth-century poison cabinet. Thank you, Silvia la Greca, for checking my Italian, and Rachel Hullett for helping me in my attempts to learn Italian.

Thank you to every bookseller and librarian who has recommended Pages & Co. to young (and not so young) readers; these books are love letters to booksellers and librarians, and it means so much that you've taken it to your hearts. Thank you also to the brilliant teachers who always do so much to champion reading for pleasure, but have had to do it with such obstacles over the last eighteen months.

Thank you to my friends and family; to my mum and dad and sister, Hester, and to the extended Kitchens and Brays. Thank you to the Cottons/Colliers/Bishops/Rices for welcoming me into your family so warmly. Thank you to my nephew,

Milo . . . this one is for you. Thank you, always, to Adam Collier for your love and for always being the first non-professionally-associated person to read my books.

Thank you to my friends, Katie Webber, Kevin Tsang, Eve Tsang, Kiran Millwood Hargrave, Tom de Freston, Cat Doyle, Jack Webber, Kate Rundell, Rosalind Jana, Paul Black, Reece Haydon Black, Rosi Crawley, Ben O'Donnell, Nicola Skinner, Francesca Gibbons, Krystal Sutherland, Chris Smith, Lizzie Morris, Sarah McKenna, Alwyn Hamilton, Laura Iredale, Ruth Heatley, Jo Kitchen, Naomi Kent, Naomi Reed, Sarah Richards, Jamie Wright, Jen Herlihy, Jon Usher, Jack Wrighton, Eric Anderson, Uli Lenart, Robyn Jankel, Matt Fairhall, and Lex Brookman.

Finally, thank you to every reader; thank you for believing in *book magic*.